HERE TO STAY

A collection of stories by women

PHYLLIS THOMPSON
IONE BROWN
EVADNEY ELLIS
LOREEN LYSEIGHT

A LION PAPERBACK

Oxford · Batavia · Sydney

Copyright © 1990 Ione Brown, Evadney Ellis, Loreen Lyseight, Phyllis Thompson

Published by
Lion Publishing plc
Sandy Lane West, Littlemore, Oxford, England
ISBN 0 7459 1829 8
Albatross Books Pty Ltd
PO Box 320, Sutherland, NSW 2232, Australia
ISBN 0 7324 0201 8

First published 1990

British Library Cataloguing in Publication Data
Here to stay.
  I. Thompson, Phyllis
  813 [F]

  ISBN 0 7459 1829 8

Printed and bound in Great Britain
by Cox & Wyman, Reading

Here to Stay

FOUR SHORT STORIES BY AFRO-CARIBBEAN WOMEN

The bitter-sweet stories in this book, all by women with Jamaican roots living in Britain, highlight significant aspects of the black experience today. Each takes readers inside the situation, to feel it for themselves, and to understand.

*Island roots are strong. Memories throw long shadows. How can those who are 'here to stay' find a place to stand between two cultures, belonging, yet living their way?

*The black church is a tower of strength, a place of shelter and community. Can a new generation keep faith as they search for a way forward?

*Parents and children, bound by strong cords of love, clash in the fight for freedom.

*How can the pain of continuing racial discrimination be channelled for a constructive future?

PHYLLIS THOMPSON, who brought the writers together on this project and has edited the book, was born in Jamaica. She has lived in England since she was nine. She is currently an Adult Education lecturer, having worked in this field since 1978. She has an active interest in the role of women in the church. All four writers have had varying involvement with the black churches. They write in the belief that there is room for hope as we face up to the realities of life.

CONTENTS

Experience flavours and colours life.
Writing captures and shapes it.

LOREEN LYSEIGHT

Memories and Shadows

IONE BROWN

Carefully and gently the palm of Pearl's left hand rested on her plump round knee. Automatically her hand moved around in an involuntary circular motion down towards the more muscular area of her short, fat, vein-strewn leg where she could feel the increasing rhythmic throbbing pain. She gently massaged and kneaded her leg until she felt the pain easing away and becoming more bearable. It seemed like a lifetime, although it was really only three and a half years, that this familiar pain had been so intensely severe. It had started in her right leg but had now graduated to her whole body. Day after day she had come to accept her lot, although she consoled herself that her Maker was still on the job.

Returning more gradually now, the pain seemed to ebb and flow throughout the whole of her right leg. Pearl lay back in the chair and allowed the movement of the pain to decrease gradually and then subside. She closed her eyes in the languor of sleep. Leaning her head against the chair-back, she experienced relief with a lull in the movement of the pain, even though experience had taught her it might be only temporary. She stretched her tired limbs and, moving her head from side to side, she felt some respite from the cramped feeling in her neck. Wearily her eyes focused on the sitting-room clock. She realized that she must have been dozing off for the last hour or so.

Slowly, and with a sense of satisfaction, her eyes took in the gold frame of the clock in all its restricted splendour. She looked around the small but comfortable room. Knowing that the comfort she now enjoyed was by no means the best, she still considered it luxurious, and it provided her with a little heaven here on earth. She fixed her gaze on the green marble coffee table and a smile gradually began at her lips. She remembered the earlier years in England and the small but welcoming bedsit that she had shared with her husband Arthur when they first arrived. People don't live like that now, she ruminated.

All the other West Indians she knew who had begun life in Britain in a similar way had had the same high expectations and most of them were just as comfortable as she was now, if not more so. But leaving the loving warm arms of the Island only to be met by the cold reception of the Motherland had resulted in shattered illusions for many. Motherland, Motherland, there's the joke. The word 'Motherland' seemed to take shape in Pearl's mind as she remembered the absence of the motherly kindness that she had hoped for.

Sitting up now so that her surroundings were more in focus, she gazed round with contented pride. She looked up into the corner of the room and eyed ruefully the damp and peeling wallpaper over the window-frame. She would have to tell David her son about this some time, and he would attend to it. It was a comforting thought to know that you had someone to call on. The velvet curtains and luxurious shag-pile carpet accentuated by the pink floral wallpaper brought a harmony to all she now saw. The room was warm and cosy and stood in a stark contrast to the bedsit with its cold unwelcoming lino flooring and paraffin heater. Her children had been totally responsible for these new comforts. In an attempt to 'modernize' their mother they had all contributed their time and modest finances to make sure she was comfortable. Having overcome her reluctance to part with her old furniture and exchange it for new, they had helped to plan the décor of her new home.

Them have too much style, these children — posh car, posh house, posh clothes, she thought, shaking her head.

The only piece of furniture that remained from the old days was the onyx-coloured formica cabinet that she refused to part with. It had been a major first purchase when she had arrived in England and it now housed the remaining bits and pieces of the dinner sets and trinkets that she had salvaged from her kitchen. A lot of these were wedding presents and were very precious. Despite its incongruous presence in this room, the cabinet was still her most prized possession. She kept this knowledge to herself, however, because she did not want her children to think that she was ungrateful for what they had done.

The street outside her window was now becoming less busy with commuters and Christmas shoppers and the darkening evening light reminded Pearl that the curtains were still undrawn. She made a forward movement with the intention of rising from the chair, but the throbbing pain in her leg increased in intensity and she could do little else but fall slowly back into the chair and close her eyes. She felt the pain rising and falling like small waves. After a while the undulation melted into small rivulets of pain. She had learnt over the years to accept this inconvenience, though not without some regret, as her personal trial. In her more light-hearted moods she even went so far as to personify its presence, addressing her intangible enemy as 'Mr Pain' and challenging the mysterious but frequent visitor to overcome her if he dare. Yes, she was all too familiar with his tactics of coming when she was least prepared and receding paradoxically when she least wanted him to, when she felt she was in control. Was she not a martyr to affliction?

She was not physically or mentally very strong and was rather a coward when it came to any kind of pain. She remembered that in her youth she feared pain intensely even before she had experienced it. Watching over her grandmother wasting away in spasms of excruciating agony before she drew her last breath had been in itself an education in suffering. But now she knew almost no fear. The sense of weakness followed by nausea that most mornings incapacitated her will to rise from her bed was so familiar that she endured discomfort with very little awareness of what she was actually feeling. Each day was an uphill struggle. Nevertheless, she was grateful for small mercies: she had not reached the bed of affliction. She could still move around her house and carry out her household duties unaided, and this sense of independence meant a lot to her.

Healing services were still important. But her legs, and especially the right one, had continued to worsen despite the medical and spiritual attention they had received. The revival meeting that she had so anxiously looked forward to on the previous evening had been a blessing. She had not been feeling at all well that day and her right leg had swollen so badly that it had become unbearable to walk on. Pearl had made up her mind that this was one meeting she would have to miss. But now she knew that she was meant to go all along. Her thoughts went back to the previous evening, and gradually she began to relive the physical and spiritual pleasure of that night. As the fervent prayer of the saints had graduated to loftier heights, she remembered moving towards the front even before the invitation to healing had been given. On her knees she persevered in prayer asking God to intervene.

'Praise God.' As the words left her lips she was barely conscious of their pronouncement.

Pastor Goodson, seeing the sincerity and depth of emotion of his sister, moved towards her, put his hands on her shoulder and joined her on her knees at the altar. All around cacophonic sounds filled the church and choruses followed by prayer and choruses again melted into one. The stamping and shouting that echoed the earnest praying and singing and the rise and fall of voices communicating in prayer went on for what seemed like hours. After a while the voices grew hoarse and the sound rose and fell with evident weariness. Slowly Pearl rose from the altar, rubbing her knees. She gradually became aware of the sweaty, wrinkled face of Pastor Goodson. 'Believe God, my sister,' he advised. His glazed eyes showed signs of a man who had not fully returned to his former consciousness. He had launched out into the deep-sea world of prayer.

Pearl's late husband Arthur had never really accepted her commitment to the Lord and to the church and he had never once shared her steady but growing faith. He was often cynical about religion in general but never openly objected to her going to church or weekday meetings. But Pearl suffered a strong sense of guilt from the fact that she often found herself excluding her husband from an area of her life that seemed to touch all others. They had shared so much together all their married life only now to experience an ever-increasing distance between them. She had tried to remain a dutiful wife. She always invited him to her church when they had special meetings and on one or two occasions, after a lot of coaxing, quarrelling and moaning, Arthur had gone. He was nevertheless very critical of what he saw there. Why did Arthur have to go on so? Pearl reflected. After all, they never do anything to him, you know.

The fact that he was now dead and had not repented of his life was at first a deeper pain than the event of his death, but with the passing of time she was learning to accept that there

14

was nothing more she could have done. Now she would have to encourage her children, if they would only listen.

She remembered the evening that was the turning-point in her life quite vividly. It was about seven years before Arthur's death, Pearl remembered, and she had now been alone for eight years. Leaving work with Linda that evening, she had phoned Arthur to tell him that she would be late because she had decided to go on to church. Linda was always inviting her to church, but it was not until that particular evening that she felt she wanted to go. She still had reservations. Apart from the few weddings, christenings and funerals that had brought her to church in Britain, there had been nothing to attract her.

But that particular evening had been a transforming experience. Not only her body but her very soul seemed to enter into the spirit of the meeting. She felt at one with the people around her: it was like being part of a family again. Her feeble attempt at trying to articulate this to Arthur and the children was miserably inadequate. 'Mum's got religion,' was their understanding of it. Yet the indelible impression of that evening was enough to convince Pearl that she had been merely the shadow of a full person before. How could she expect Arthur or the children to understand?

It had always been Pearl who had insisted on going to church with Arthur in the early days, during their courtship and subsequent marriage. She enjoyed the sermons of Pastor Beckford who had fathered the main district church on the Island and who had also married them. At least once a month she would insist that a morning in church with her man and child was where she should be. She was then only a church-goer. As she walked through the district on her way to church the sound of sacred music came from the homes of dwellers far and wide and echoed throughout the hills. Those who did not have record players or tape recorders sang aloud their favourite hymn. Few people, if they had any God in them, would allow secular music to be played in their house on Sundays. It did not matter that the same Jim Reeves record was played religiously week after week. Even if you were not a regular church attender, respect for the Sabbath was equated with respect due

15

to employers or elders. Both Pearl and Arthur acquiesced to this blind observance.

Looking back to that time in her life, Pearl realized that it was probably unfair to have expected Arthur to understand the way her life had changed, because she did not understand it herself. However, the strained silence in the house that seemed to permeate the very air she breathed after that evening disappointed and disheartened her. The silence was acute, and she remembered feeling that it was a lot more significant than anything that could have been said.

Pearl sighed. The slow steady process of unravelling her life was at times more painful than physical pain. Sometimes she felt that the whole experience was a mere dream and that she would one day wake out of it to face the knowing ridicule of her family and their cynicism. After a while these worries took second place to the uncertainty and doubt that occupied her thoughts.

Was that me, Pearl? she had asked herself many times.

Looking back at her unregrettable conviction and the many trials and tribulations she had overcome, she was certain now that it was. Arthur's refusal to accept or even listen to anything she had to say about what was happening to her had been unbearably painful at first. Uncharacteristically he had exuded an air of indifference that began to erode Pearl's newfound confidence. Then she reached a point where she knew she could bear it no longer. She had to confront the situation.

She remembered vividly now that Saturday evening. The children had gone out to their various evening entertainments. Arthur himself was getting ready to go out on his usual Saturday-night visits. He was never a pub man and the informal gathering of family and friends was enough to meet his need for socializing. That particular evening he was planning to visit his sister Doreen who had recently come out of hospital.

Pearl remembered feeling a strong sense of guilt. She had always gone with Arthur to visit sick relatives and friends and she felt that she ought to accompany him. It was true that she had very rarely visited Doreen, but on that particular evening she felt more than ever a sense of duty. Arthur was standing in

16

the hall and, as usual before he went out, he was taking time to scrutinize himself in the full-length hall mirror. Pearl often laughed inwardly and asked herself how many times she had seen him go through this narcissistic routine that was one of his many idiosyncrasies.

Pearl mused on. A picture of Arthur's familiar face and frame now surfaced fully in her mind: the oval-shaped sugar-brown face, the warm and slanted eyes and the meticulously-groomed black shiny eyebrows. The walrus moustache was an acquisition that Arthur had taken pride in since he was a youth back home on the Island. Many of the girls in the district had been attracted to his good looks, not least Pearl. A dapper man with the wisdom of age and experience now stood before her. He took pride in his appearance, always insisting on a clean white shirt.

'A dry island tourist, that man,' Pearl mouthed affectionately to herself. Always in the habit of overdressing for social gatherings, he rendered his wife a poor relation. However, Pearl did not mind. She was and would always be proud of him. Many West Indian men of Arthur's age did not take enough interest in themselves and they had lost all sense of self-worth. It was true that living in Britain had taken away a lot of youthful enthusiasm and energy, but through it all one had to be resilient. Arthur had been.

From her position in the kitchen Pearl could see him still adjusting his tie. She watched him for a while, waiting for the right moment to mention what had been unmentionable for many weeks. Some kind of confrontation, though unfamiliar and undesirable, was now inevitable. Pearl had to unburden herself.

'So what's wrong, Arthur? You don't want me to go out . . . to church?'

She could hear her voice tremble and, clearing the build-up of phlegm from her throat, she pressed her now stiffened lips tighter together as a means of having some control over her next utterance. She had not thought to say this first. She had intended to sound confident and calm. Now she felt disappointed. Her next utterance would be more guarded and controlled, she told herself. After all, why should she sound nervous? She had done nothing to be ashamed of.

She was glad that she was so near the kitchen sink unit and she leaned against it for physical support. Arthur continued to straighten an already perfectly-adjusted tie. She knew that he was not in a receptive frame of mind. He would not want to discuss anything with her, especially now that he was preparing to leave the house. Still she pressed on. Slowly she moved towards him. It was an involuntary movement because her thoughts did not seem to be moving with her. Arthur continued to adjust his tie as though oblivious of her presence. She had begun to repeat her question, knowing full well that it did not fall on deaf ears, when Arthur interjected, cutting her short.

'Listen, I never stop you from doing what you want, you hear, so don't bother me.' His voice was dismissive.

He continued to look in the mirror as he talked. As yet there had been no eye-to-eye contact, only two voices one after the other falling and rising in the space between them. Pearl knew that what her husband had said was true. Unlike many of the women she knew, whose husbands insisted on accounting for their every movement, her husband did not put reins on her. She eyed him inquisitively, trying to formulate her next verbal response. The seemingly-impregnable façade could be dismantled. She stood looking at him intently. He could be a hard man at times, a bit of a rough diamond.

She watched helplessly Arthur's hurried movements as he put on his overcoat and hat, took his umbrella and left the house without another word. The cold metallic sound of the catch was the concluding remark to their brief domestic encounter, and in the house there hung a dumb silence. Pearl remained standing against the kitchen doorpost. After a while she was aware of an increase in her rate of breathing and before she was able to take a firm grip of herself round, salty tears began to well up in the corners of her eyes and flow down her cheeks towards tightly-closed lips, which seemed to form a barrier against them. The more she tried to hold back the tears the more copiously they flowed. She refused to be broken. It was going to be a fight, she knew now, but she knew she would overcome because

18

she was not alone. Then she allowed the tears to flow more freely.

Of course it had taken a while for Arthur to adjust to this new woman his wife had become, and over the years he grew less taciturn and more responsive. There were times when he even went to the trouble, albeit in jest, to remind her of her duty as a Christian to be an example and a light to the family. He was never one to verbalize his feelings, but years of marriage to him had allowed Pearl some understanding of the approval he wanted to show, however awkwardly he expressed it. They had been through bad patches before.

What a man! Pearl's eyes smiled as she thought of her youngest daughter Janet, who was very much like her father — so much so that memories of him were painfully revived when they had their confrontations. Like her father, Janet could be extremely stubborn.

The rhythmic tick-tocking sound of the clock moving in unison with her own breathing brought Pearl back to a conscious awareness of her surroundings. She was alone in the house.

The Pentecostal Holiness Church that had begun as Pearl's second home now seemed to have become the centre of her little world. After eight years of being alone, having overcome many personal trials in her temporal and spiritual life, there remained uncharted experiences. It was at times like these that she had time to think, to reflect and to take stock. These moments were precious. Reflection was never possible when the children were around. She still welcomed the frequent visits they dutifully paid, but the church and the brethren had filled the once-vacant place that longed for a sense of belonging. The children and memories of Arthur took second place.

I have an anchor
that keeps the soul
steadfast and sure

Pearl began to sing out the chorus of her favourite hymn, of which the words had been a constant inspiration and a lifebuoy. It was only by the anchor that she had kept her hold.

Now that most of the children had grown up and, in a way, grown away from her to live their own lives there was a sense of satisfaction and assurance at having tried and done her best. Their formative years had been a struggle compounded by their move to England. This had particularly affected her two eldest daughters Evette and Lorraine. They were now set up in their own flats and seemed to be coping well. From time to time she looked after Lorraine's four-year-old son Desmond while her daughter was at work. He was certainly a handful, but his cheeky smile and lively intelligence compensated for the misdemeanours that kept Pearl on her toes when she looked after him.

She wished that Lorraine had not become a mother so early. She was an intelligent girl who had a promising career with the bank before falling pregnant. Now just twenty-two and saddled with a young child whose need for attention during his waking hours constantly had to be met she had very little time for herself. At the same age Pearl herself had been the mother of two children, but she had had Arthur to look after her and had expectations of marriage. Still that was life. You can't send children back because they are inconvenient.

Her worries for Janet had lessened as she had watched her develop from an insecure rebellious youth to the entrepreneurial young lady that she now was. With some of her savings Pearl had helped Janet to get started in her own fashion-design business and had watched the business grow from strength to strength. She had more confidence now in Janet than in any of her other children — she was so levelheaded. She had known at an early age what she wanted from life but had gone the wrong way about getting it by leaving home at a vulnerable age. Yet she was now back at home.

Whatever had happened had happened and Pearl comforted herself with the thought that she had brought her children up as best she could. She had made herself available as far as was possible when they needed her and did so even now.

20

The caller must have been ringing for some time because now the person was pushing the bell repeatedly and showing signs of impatience at being left to wait. Pearl was brought back to the present by the sound. Making her way towards the hall, she wondered who the caller might be.

Sis Russel looked tired as she ambled into the sitting-room with Bible and brown leather handbag firmly clutched in her right hand. She was out of breath and was glad to be in the warm out of the cold night air. She had made it her duty to visit her beloved sister Pearl in order to strengthen and encourage where she saw the need. At all times she was armed with 'the word', the salient parts of which she had committed to memory as a young woman but now found she could not recall at will. Instead she would read from the leather-bound King James Bible that was her closest and constant companion. Having survived the stifling stench of urine and acidic-smelling alcohol at the pub on the corner of Tanner Street, Sis Russel had braved her way through the groups of aimless youths who met religiously every evening around that location to exchange drinks, drugs and puerile tales of their happy hours. They seemed to be the natural enemy of morally-upright citizens and to Sis Russel their very presence was repugnant. She had quickened her pace as she passed them.

Now settling into Pearl's armchair was a rather buxom domesticated-looking woman whose eyes seemed to mirror the struggles, trials and temptations she had overcome. Her fifty-five years of life seemed more like sixty-five with the weight of unspoken domestic problems. The thin wrinkled crow's feet around her wizened eyes and lips seemed to tell a meaningful life story. She allowed herself to smile very rarely unless she felt it embarrassing not to, such as at christenings and weddings. She was used to people unburdening themselves in her presence, yet she never felt the need to unburden herself. Both in and out of her church circle she was the epitome of the maternal — spiritual and physical mother. She exuded an air of all-knowing that instinctively drew the burdened to her.

'Then how are you, Sister Pearl?' Sis Russel enquired as she made herself comfortable in the chair that Pearl had so

21

contentedly occupied before her friend's arrival. Pearl did not mind giving up a seat for such a good friend. As always, her sitting-room was cosy and welcoming. Many of her friends had said this even though they themselves kept up sitting-rooms garishly embellished with small ornaments and cluttered up with large brightly-coloured crochets and fancy fur rugs. Those rooms were not for their visitors but were retained more as museums or sanctuaries. But Pearl's sitting-room was well used as she now spent a lot of her time here either watching the television or knitting. It seemed to be the most appropriate place in the house. In the winter there was always a warm fire and in the summer the room was always full of sunlight.

The two women had become good friends since Pearl had become a member of the Pentecostal Holiness Church and they always looked forward to the evenings spent together reminiscing about their cares in life and the chances that had escaped them. There was also an opportunity to exchange the latest church gossip. Yet recently they had simply been content to enjoy the silent presence between them. Sis Russel had seemed to be unusually pensive and unresponsive and Pearl had tried to be sensitive to this mood. Confidantes? It seemed that their relationship was more superficial than real and yet they consolidated their faith during these encounters and parted company strengthened to endure a little more.

One could not fail to have a certain amount of respect for this woman, as indeed Pearl had. She seemed to command it by her very presence. Pearl cringed with secret embarrassment every time she was invited to drop the use of the more formal 'Sis Russel' that came to her lips more readily than 'Esther'. The church was not like the world and a certain modicum of respect for one's spiritual superiors must be shown. To become so familiar was tantamount to trespassing on forbidden territory. Sis Russel's experience of spiritual and temporal warfare far surpassed her own and from her she had a lot to learn. She knew very little about her friend's private life, as she rarely discussed it, but she knew that she had overcome many temporal battles in her own private affairs, although the nature of them was not quite clear. She knew that her husband had left the family home when the children were still quite young and recently she had heard from some source that he had remarried. Sis Russel's two youngest children she knew by sight only. Raymond and Christine had been Janet's young companions in the church before they had all decided to leave. Pearl did not know what had become of them as Janet no longer saw them and Sis Russel never mentioned them.

'I'm not too bad, Sister Russel. You know how it go already.'

Sis Russel, with her usual perception, knew that Pearl was on her own.

'Where's Janet, she gan out?'

'Yes, she say she gan do some shopping.'

'She not working today?'

'No, she have someone working in the shop for her now, you know,' Pearl said enthusiastically. 'The business doing really well.'

'She still a-talk to the Rasta-man?'

The question was a means of diverting the conversation away from Janet's success, which was not what Sis Russel wanted to hear about. On her last visit she had been unfortunate enough to meet Janet's young man Clive and she could not say that she was at all impressed. At least Janet did not seem to be the least bit interested in the religion her boyfriend followed. But still Sis Russel disapproved and she made this quite clear. Pearl had very little to say on the matter. Janet was, after all, old enough to choose her own friends. She had gone to church with her mother on a couple of occasions but had not shown any sign of making a decision about her religious allegiance.

'When God come, medear, she can't say she never was introduced to him, Pearl.'

Sis Russel was sincere. Young people today were allowed far too much freedom, and far too many parents, including West Indian parents, were allowing their children to do their own thing with consequences that were all too familiar. In their own church Sis Russel had been the instigator of many battles, setting up old against young and men against women. Anything that there was to criticize she would be the first to criticize. The music and the style of clothes all came under her close scrutiny.

Now fully ensconced, she allowed her large round body to sink into the chair more fully. She slowly stretched out her brown stocking-clad legs to rest in a position where she could feel the warmth of the fire on them.

'I don't know what she see in that boy. Him have religion though?' She sucked air through her teeth in disgust. 'Janet must know what she doing, man.'

'Him say that he's not a Rasta . . . that what him a-do is follow the . . . me no remember what him say now . . . but him no deep into the thing if you understand what I mean. Sometime he even go to that church down the road.' Pearl did not want to take Clive or Janet's side but she was trying to be fair.

'What you say? The church down the road? Near the row of shops? Then tell me, Pearl, can the Spirit take up residence there?'

Pearl did not quite know how to answer this question. Judging by the look Sis Russel was giving she was sure it was not rhetorical but required an immediate answer that would confirm her friend's point of view. She raised her hand up in the air with a forced look of bewilderment. Sis Russel would read this gesture as seconding her own thoughts.

'I remember when I came to England, Pearl,' Sis Russel continued, 'and made it my duty to go and find a church to worship and I can't say I find one where my soul could say yes. Pearl, the looks alone . . . '

As she talked she began to sit more upright in the chair so that her face was level with that of her listener. Pearl observed her friend's movements as she talked and could not deny that what she had said was true. That initial feeling of rejection was far too well remembered. She too had not expected nor been able to comprehend the xenophobic reception that greeted them on their arrival. She was saddened by the white people she met who made it quite clear that she was not welcome but she had concluded that they were probably not Christians. Her visit to the local church proved to be a rude awakening.

It was so hard to understand. Back home the church was always such a welcoming place. And after all, had she not come to Britain as an invited visitor? She remembered the many radio broadcasts and even television programmes encouraging West Indians to come to the so-called Motherland. It was their country too. This they had been led to believe by assurances given by the government. So Pearl and Arthur had brought forward their wedding as soon as they were certain of their tickets and shortly after that arrived in Britain: young, married and expectant of a good future. The ice-cold welcome and manufactured plastic smiles had been disheartening for a while. After a time Pearl and Arthur began to read through the knowing looks and smiles.

Pearl's mind straddled her thoughts of the past and of her present situation. The two women sat in silence, unconscious of each other's thoughts and listening to the sounds of their own breathing. Pearl looked at the clock and watched the minute hand at five and then ten minutes past seven. It had slipped her mind that she was going to put the kettle on, because Janet would be in soon and would probably want a cup of tea herself. No sooner had this thought left her mind than she heard the familiar sound of the key in the front door.

Closing the door quietly behind her, Janet slowly removed her scarf and coat. She hung them over the coat-rail in the meticulous way she handled all her clothes. Adjusting her hair and jumper, she made her way towards the sitting-room and recognized the voice that answered her mother's invitation to a cup of tea. It was strange that Sis Russel should be here tonight. Janet had not expected to see her until some time later in the week when she was planning to pay her an unexpected personal visit.

As Janet came further into the room she was very conscious of a critical eye noting her every movement. The concentration on her made Janet feel as though she were being swallowed. She went over to the window to draw the curtain and then over to the settee where she sat opposite the armchair occupied by their visitor. She felt the warm air around her seeping slowly into her cold flesh. It was always a good feeling to come home on winter evenings. Having waited nearly an hour for her bus she now felt grateful and relieved.

From her chair Sis Russel continued to stare at Janet. She felt uneasy in her presence and especially so now that Pearl was not in the room. She could hear her friend moving around purposefully in the kitchen. Part of the discomfort was the picture that was now becoming so clear in her mind. Christine, Christine. Why did Janet always remind her so much of Christine?

The last time she had seen her daughter was five years ago and even her name was upsetting. Christine had left home ignominiously, a mere teenager who was seven months pregnant. The shame and disgrace that this had brought on the family and her mother in particular was too painful to remember. After the rigid puritanical line that Sis Russel had so diligently pursued in the upbringing of her children, especially during their teenage years, she now lived with bitter shame.

She remembered the clandestine meetings and the arguments that followed Christine's determination to continue her relationship with Leroy. Evening after evening the house seemed to echo to the sound of the voices of mother and daughter raised in heated exchanges as one helplessly tried to uphold what she saw as a certain standard in her home and the other defended her right to her independence.

After a while things had calmed down and Sis Russel had come to terms with the pregnancy but not with Leroy. How could such a good-for-nothing young man presume on her good nature? Her lips pursed as the memories surfaced. Even now there was no remorse. After five years the gap between her and her daughter seemed to have widened. Christine had sensed this at the start and had recognized that there was no option but to make up her mind not to have anything more to do with her family. Not even Raymond had taken her side. Leroy had promised to stand by her but without a job there was little hope of fulfilling many of the promises he had made. Sis Russel bit her lips slowly as she looked up at Janet again. Why did she remind her so much of Christine?

It was sad the way that her daughter's life had so closely mirrored her own. Her thoughts went back thirty-five years to the Island and the time when she too had so unexpectedly become a mother. Everton her son was the living proof. She was sure that she had made the right decision to leave him and come to England to join her sister but she had not done so without deep regrets. For many years she had suppressed the memory of her banishment from the church and subsequent ostracism from the people she had let down. She had paid a dear price. The district people had been so spiteful and cruel and her ticket to England had seemed like a mirage in a desert. There were many single mothers like herself but not many of them had fallen so disgracefully. Such behaviour had not been expected of her.

Now in England and with a failed marriage behind her she had striven to provide the best for her children and to guide them away from the kind of life she had experienced first hand. Christine was the most vulnerable because she was a girl and it was with good intentions that she had sought to protect her. If only she had stayed, just listened, taken some advice . . .

Slowly the memories of the past began to erase themselves from her mind. Sis Russel looked at Janet again but this time even more intently. It was almost as if she knew something even though she did not. The room seemed to have become very warm and the air felt dry. Sis Russel cleared her throat and opened the two top buttons of her cardigan. The close atmosphere was now making her feet sweaty and uncomfortable in her shoes. Usually she would have removed her shoes by now but somehow she did not feel that she could.

Janet was unusually quiet. It was not the past that occupied her mind. Her thoughts were troubled by the day's event. Could it be just a coincidence? While shopping that afternoon she had vaguely recognized an old friend and had walked up to her in disbelief. She was surprised to see Christine after such a long time. They had met as children when their mothers had made them go to church and they had also been at college together. Janet remembered that Christine had left half-way through the year. They had never been close friends but seemed always to have something to talk about.

After exchanging some news about themselves and mutual acquaintances they discovered that neither of them was particularly busy that day. Janet was taking time off from the boutique. Christine had been cooped up in her flat with her two children and when they had become too boisterous she had decided that they should all take a walk to the shops. Anyway, there was very little food in the flat. Now she stood clutching two plastic bags of shopping and talking to Janet while her two children clung to her possessively and busy Christmas shoppers jostled around them. Christine chatted away excitedly but the worn expression in her tired eyes was evident. She seemed to have reached a point where the last vestiges of her youth had faded. She suffered a recurrent depression that cast a shadow over her.

Janet wanted to continue the conversation and suggested that they go to a local café. Christine agreed enthusiastically but was stunned with embarrassment when the young waitress came to ask for their orders. As usual she had only just enough money for the rest of the week and was reluctant to spend it. Janet's offer to pay was a relief that she could only accept gratefully.

Christine now felt humbled in Janet's presence. She remembered their college days. It was she who had commanded attention then and not Janet. Now she could not remember the last time when she had been invited to sit down to a drink or a meal of any kind. Those luxuries seemed to belong in the past. Leroy had never had much money and when the second child arrived they had to account carefully for every penny.

As she sat looking at Janet her eyes began to take in the meticulously-groomed appearance and the fresh liveliness and carelessness of youth. This only served to bring out more intensely her feeling of wretchedness and she sought to suppress it by feigning enthusiasm to shield her secret hurt. If life had been different perhaps she could have been in Janet's position. She and Leroy had had so many hopes and dreams for the future when they met. They had planned to do so much together and success seemed still to be within reach even after

28

the birth of the first child. She had had hope then and she realized that now she had none.

When they had no more information to exchange the talk became more and more inconsequential. While seats in the café became vacant one by one the world outside became busier by the second as shoppers laden with Christmas bags made their way home. The children were becoming restless. They eyed the stranger who had taken away their mother's attention. Instinctively they liked her. After learning their names Janet had winked at them several times and was rewarded with two sunny smiles. Despite their dishevelled appearance they were two very beautiful children and their mother was obviously proud of them.

Christine reflected on her account of the last five years. In that time she had had no contact with her family. Now that she had returned to the area she was reluctant to contact them. Five years of guilt had plagued her and the hard experiences of her life had contributed nothing to heal her wounds. It had been so difficult even to entertain the thought of making amends after so long. She had left so confident of success but had finally resolved to admit her mistake for the sake of her children even if not for her own. Her own experience had made her aware of the life her mother had suffered after her father had absconded and left them to the mercy of the state. She now knew that her mother's obduracy and insensitivity had been a safety mechanism. Yet her mother had had her faith to strengthen her. What did she have? Surely it was only a matter of time before she took leave of her sanity.

The exchanges between the two girls became less lively and a look of spent exhilaration could be read on their faces. Time had passed quickly and the afternoon was drawing to a close. Desmond was fast asleep in his mother's arms and Tony busied himself with observing the passers-by and the brightly-lit shop windows. He attempted to draw his mother's attention to what he saw but he received only rebukes to sit still.

It felt so strange to be sitting there together. They grew pensive. In the silence, Christine wondered whether or not she dared to share her worries with her friend. The pauses in the conversation grew longer and seemed to urge her to confess her real concerns. But she could not. Suddenly she realized that Janet was looking out of the window and preparing to leave.

'Janet, before you go, will you do something for me?' The words seemed to come from her lips uncontrolled.

Janet looked at Christine curiously and wondered what she could be asking her to do.

'My mum . . . ' Christine went on. The word 'mum' coming from her own lips sounded so strange now. She was so used to being called 'Mum' by her own children. 'Well, I suppose you realize by now that I have not seen her for a long time and . . . I really would like to . . . get in contact with her. I wonder if . . . ' The words were slow and hesitantly delivered.

Before Janet had had a chance to absorb fully what she might be asked to do, Christine was hunting around in her bag. She drew out a crumpled brown paper envelope and quickly scribbled her name and telephone number on the back. She handed it to Janet.

'Can you?'

'Don't worry, I'll see what I can do,' Janet replied as she got up from her chair and gathered her things together.

Christine watched her as she left the café and disappeared out of sight.

Sitting down now with the thoughts of the day's meeting so vividly in her mind, Janet felt weighed down. The woman who was sitting in front of her seemed to be more accessible. The flaws were no longer hidden. Christine had allowed Janet to see a side to Sis Russel that was so closely guarded its very existence would be doubted. She was human after all. The obdurate façade was beginning to melt.

The door opened and Pearl came over to the coffee table in the middle of the room balancing the tray in one hand and a plate of biscuits in the other. She poured out three cups of tea and allowed her visitor and her daughter to help themselves to milk and sugar. From the kitchen she had strained her ears to listen to any conversation that might take place in her absence. She knew now that both Janet and Sister Russel

30

had been unusually quiet. The sitting-room clock chimed the half hour and the reverberation lingered on, partially erasing the sound of the china cups and saucers as they clicked against each other. After a few minutes the familiar silence of the house and the quiet breathing of the room's occupants resumed its place. There seemed to be nothing to say as they sipped at the hot tea. The biscuits were left untouched.

Reaching over towards her bag, Janet felt for the envelope that she had been asked to deliver. She had not expected to do this so soon but the moment seemed to be appropriate. She knew that the longer it was left the more reluctant she would be to carry out her promise. Recalling the look in Christine's eyes was enough to convince her that now was the time. To procrastinate would not be fair either to mother or daughter.

'I saw Christine today, Sis Russel.' The words were unchecked and she uttered them in a matter-of-fact way.

Pearl had been lifting her cup to her lips but she now returned it firmly to the saucer. Sis Russel looked up at Janet incredulously. She had not quite understood what Janet had said and was unsure if the information was meant for her. But the name 'Christine' had caught her attention and made her look more keenly.

'I saw her today,' Janet continued. 'In the High Street. She asked me to give you this.' The matter-of-fact tone now became more tentative. Opening out her hand to reveal more clearly the brown envelope, Janet stood up and walked over to Sis Russel to put the paper in her hands. No hand reached out to receive it. With both hands still resting on her lap, Sis Russel looked down slowly at the paper. She bent her head closer to her lap to read the envelope. Typed on one side was the name 'Miss C. Russel' and an address that she did not recognize. She picked up the envelope and turned it over. The scribbled hand simply read 'Christine' and gave a telephone number. Slowly and silently tears formed in her eyes and rolled down her cheeks.

'You say . . . she give you this to . . . give me?'

Janet nodded.

'She aright, she remem . . . ber me?' Her enquiry was slow and muffled.

31

Sis Russel seemed to have halved in size. Taking her handkerchief from her cardigan sleeve she began to wipe her face. Her hand moved purposefully around the tear-stained face as she tried to gain control of herself. Despite the wiping her face was still covered with tears. She made curious downward grimaces with her mouth in further efforts to overcome her emotion but the imperturbability she had shown so often was gone.

'Where she deh? Where she deh?' came the muffled question. She looked up at Pearl.

'I'm a bad mother, I know, Pearl,' she said pleading for confirmation. 'I know Christine must hate me but I thought it was the right thing to do. Is not easy bringing children up on you own, Pearl, it wasn't easy. She did let me down. She let the family down, me one daughter, Pearl.' She cried uncontrollably as she tried to get the words out and after a while they became inaudible.

Pearl moved towards her friend who now seemed to want to be comforted.

'Don't worry, don't worry, Esther, you do you best. Never mind, girl, never mind.'

The furrows set deeper into her friend's face as she buried her head and cried even more profusely into the fold of her cotton skirt. Her choked sobs drew from her friend a deep sense of pity and sympathy that she had not felt for anyone in a long time.

When the clock chimed nine Sis Russel rose from her chair. Pearl looked at Janet. It was hard to allow her to walk home on her own.

'You'd better walk her home, Janet,' Pearl said softly. Janet nodded and rose to her feet. She put on her coat and helped Sister Russel into hers. As they turned into Tanner Street Janet linked arms with Sis Russel and, meeting with little resistance, moved closer to her. They walked together for the rest of their journey without saying anything to each other. There did not seem to be anything to say. Outside Sister Russel's own house they stopped and Janet waited for her to go in.

'You think I should ring her tonight?'

'No. Leave it until tomorrow. You might wake the children.'

'Children? Which children?'

'Tony and Desmond.'

'Is two she have now? I have two grandchildren?'

'Yes. They're lovely kids,' Janet confirmed.

Sister Russel smiled. It was so strange to see her smile. For so long she had had little to smile about and the smile that rested on her face now was significant.

'Goodnight, dear.' She turned and went into her house, closing the door quietly behind her and leaving Janet to make her way home. She felt for the first time in five years like a mother again.

Pearl sat waiting for her daughter to return. She did not want to go upstairs on her own. She hated being alone after having company. It was now a quarter to ten.

'Mum, are you going to bed now?'

Pearl looked up at Janet. She had not heard her come in. Her eyes focused on her daughter. It was surprising how much you missed when you were deep in thought.

'Give me your arm, Janet. I don't know if I can get up, me legs dem cramp up.'

Upstairs, as she unlaced her girdle and prepared herself for bed, she became conscious of her aching limbs and eyes. She put on her nightdress and her headscarf. Once she was in bed she felt the tiredness of the day releasing itself from her limbs. She prayed her usual prayer and settled her body in its usual position for sleep. Sleep was not forthcoming. She lay still for a while, trying to make out the familiar shapes of her furniture in the dark room, trying to empty her mind of the day's thoughts. This too was difficult. She could hear the sound of Janet's quiet movements in the room next door. She turned over slowly and switched on the bedside lamp. Her thoughts went back to the evening's event. She did not quite understand it all. She knew one thing, though. Her friend was not going to be the same again. It was surprising how well one knew a person and yet

33

did not know them. Disjointed thoughts of their friendship began to drift to and fro in her mind and sleep came quietly and peacefully.

'Mum, Mum, wake up . . . Mum!'

Beside her bed she could see Janet in the darkened room. Pearl was still not fully awake. The radio alarm clock read 8.35. It was too early to get up. Why was Janet now trying to wake her up?

'What is it?' Pearl asked with her head still on the pillow.

'Raymond, he's just phoned, Mum . . . '

'Raymond? Which Raymond?' Pearl was now quite confused. Janet did not seem to be making any sense.

'You know, Raymond, Sis Russel's son. He said . . . he said . . . ' Janet's eyes by now had filled with tears, and her next few words were uttered between sobs of shock and grief.

'He said she died. Sister Russel died in her sleep last night.'

Tangled Lives
PHYLLIS THOMPSON

Jessica lay in the dark. Her body, mind and spirit tossed, twirled and became increasingly thwarted by her inability to sleep. She willed the tears to ease her of her grief and shame, but her mind refused to co-operate. She rolled over onto her back, placed her hands behind her head and watched the fragmented memory of the ignoble events of the evening unfold before her mind's eye like a bad dream.

She could hear Mother Walters' strong voice declaring to the congregation, as she did habitually, 'Brothers and Sisters, I stand to report victory in the name of Jesus.' In her effort to publicise her weekly success story of how she 'overcame the old dragon whose duty till Jesus comes is to tempt the children of God,' Mother Walters invariably quoted choruses and Bible verses, as if her own words would invalidate her testimony. This Sunday evening was no exception. She moved out of her seat as she spoke.

Jessica remembered looking at her attire, noting the brown felt hat covering almost all of her greying hair and secured by the same old hat pin. The only other accessory Mother Walters allowed herself, 'because it serves a practical purpose', was her gold watch. The cream cardigan that hung from her shoulders matched her home-made cream-and-brown Sunday-best skirt, which dangled between her ankles and calf, 'an example of sobriety for the young'.

'Brethren,' her voice continued in Jessica's head, 'we are fighting a spiritual battle, you know.' As she spoke, the brothers and sisters uttered affirmative 'Amens' and 'Oh, yes ma'am' and 'Thank you, Jesus', confirming their perception and experience of the battle: every move, every victory, every defeat. The details could be omitted. They too were in the fight like one mighty army.

Sister Mary followed Mother Walters. She started to sing and asked everyone to join in because the song told her testimony.

the hotter the battle, the sweeter the victory . . .

The chorus was repeated for what must have been the third or fourth time, and the stamping, clapping and body swaying to the jubilant sounds of tambourines, drums and guitars became more pronounced. The words of the chorus were almost overwhelmed as the congregation united in its celebration of triumph.

Jessica remembered her uncomfortable involvement. It wasn't that she doubted the reality of the triumph or that she had no victory to report. She simply did not feel part of the spiritual drama and did not particularly wish to fake enthusiasm. She had maintained her reserve before, and no one had noticed — or at least no one had commented. She shuddered as the picture of the evening continued to unfold.

By this time many of the brethren were dancing up and down the aisles or jumping about in their pews. Jessica's daughter, Fou-Fou, was sound asleep on the bench with her coat rolled under her head for a pillow. Jessica was standing and mouthing the words of the song. Her mind was miles away and she certainly never saw Mother Walters moving towards her. All she knew was that Mother Walters had pulled her out from the pew and proceeded to lead her to the altar, bawling and calling on Jesus as she went.

The memory of the hot and cold flush of embarrassment made Jessica seethe with anger. Anger at Mother Walters and anger at herself. She remembered how she had struggled with her inner reluctance to co-operate with Mother Walters' demands to 'cry out Jesus', and how she had complied out of respect for authority in her church. Now that she was out of the situation, she asked herself why she had allowed Mother Walters to subjugate her and why she had not made a run for the exit. She could have asked Mother Walters to explain why she had picked on her, asked her to justify her actions, even though that would have contravened common practice.

The tears welled up in Jessica's eyes as she imagined the stares and conclusions of those watching her back and burning ears as she knelt at the altar in obedience. The tears streamed down the sides of her cheeks onto her arms and pillow. It might have helped if someone had talked about the incident with her afterwards, but nobody said anything. The nearest people got to comment was, 'Sister Jessica, I will be praying for you,' as they gave the customary handshake. She lacked the courage to defy convention and ask her well-wishers just what in particular they would be praying about. She had left the church well vexed.

Eventually, the burden of her memory was overwhelmed by sleep. When she opened her eyes it was morning and Fou-Fou was standing by the side of her bed looking down at her.

'It's breakfast time, Mum.' Fou-Fou spoke in a voice which rarely allowed Jessica any alternative than to lift her four-year-old bundle of joy and cuddle her before answering.

Whenever Jessica was summoned to breakfast by Fou-Fou's demand instead of by the alarm clock, the morning could be expected to be chaotic. This morning was no exception. Fou-Fou felt that the morning was for her to organize. She wanted Rice Krispies for breakfast, and her imaginary friend, Tosh, wanted Frosties. Jessica calmly explained to Fou-Fou that there was just about enough time to eat, have a quick wash and, if they were lucky, get to Marsden Prep before 9 a.m. Fortunately, Fou-Fou's hair was cane-rowed to last the week. Jessica silently thanked God for her job as a community librarian, which fitted in well around Fou-Fou's day. Filled with thoughts, she went to sit down with her bowl of muesli.

'Mum, you'll squash him!' Fou-Fou shrieked.

Before Jessica knew it, the tiled kitchen floor was covered with pieces of crockery, cereal and milk. She closed her eyes and suppressed her annoyance: 'Whatever things are pure, good and lovely, think on these,' she said to herself. She glared at Fou-Fou, who was sitting with her eyes and mouth agape.

'Who would I have squashed?' Jessica asked, her voice quiet and controlled.

'Tosh, of course,' replied Fou-Fou convincingly. 'He was sitting quietly in case you changed your mind and gave him some Frosties.'

Jessica shook her head and sighed. 'You have five minutes to finish your breakfast, which is about as long as it will take me to clear up some of this mess. We will then have to move at the speed of lightning to get you to school and me to work on time.'

The day's work went surprisingly quickly. Jessica spent most of the morning persuading her borough council to release funds for the appointment of a resident children's writer who could develop a story-telling workshop for parents as well as a writing project for parents and children. She was feeling proud of herself because she had also won in the war of words: the job advertisement would carry the line, 'The writer will be expected to have an interest in parents and children in the neighbourhood whose backgrounds and culture are under-represented in published work.'

As she mused on her success, her mind brought her back to the night before. Her countenance changed. The events seemed so remote from the reality of her day. The power she wielded at work and in her home contrasted with the passive way she behaved at church. She thought about Mother Walters' position and the power the local church allowed her to exercise and she thought about how emotional Mother Walters could become. Perhaps Mother Walters had got swept along by the tide of the Spirit and had decided to use Jessica as a prop to show others not moved by the tide that the altar was the diving-board. Mother Walters' logic and behaviour did not always 'suit the reasoning of men', the elders would claim, further mystifying her conduct.

God knows, Jessica reminded herself. God knows I've done nothing wrong. After all, I've tried very hard to live 'the holy life' since I returned to the church four years ago. I moved out of Clive's flat in obedience to the teachings, since he wasn't prepared to marry me. God, you've been good to Fou-Fou and me. Jessica looked up as if God was looking down at her. She counselled herself as she always did when she thought of Fou-Fou's father: 'Abraham had a lamb provided in the thicket, but for you, Jessy girl, God requires the full sacrifice.' Jessica sighed, half in despair of the issue and half at her realization of how she depended on biblical images and gospel songs to think about and make sense of many of her experiences.

The chimes of the town hall clock across the road were a feature of Jessica's workday. She checked her watch and organized herself to go home. Travelling home from work and picking up

Fou-Fou were done with the automation that comes with routine.

Bathing Fou-Fou was a daily event that Jessica appreciated. It wasn't so much the delight of watching Fou-Fou's pleasure as she obeyed her daughter's demands to pour buckets of water over her, nor was it totally to do with the therapeutic relaxation the occasion offered her after her day's work. It was more that these moments with her daughter enabled the cultivation of a harmony between herself and Fou-Fou that had come too late between her own mother and herself.

Jessica also believed fervently that she owed it to the next generation to pass on the sense of black pride that she had discovered far too late in her own life. She was starting with Fou-Fou. Bathtimes were followed by bedtime stories of African folk tales or, more frequently, made-up stories that they would weave about a drawing or photograph of a particular black person or scene. Jessica kept notes of the ideas they created. One day, she hoped, she would be able to develop the stories for publication. As usual, she was motivated by a forceful ambition. However, this evening's talk-story would have to be brief because Jessica was going out to one of her twice-a-year meetings and she wanted Fou-Fou to go to sleep before the baby-minder arrived.

Tonight, the starting-point for the talk-story was one of last year's Christmas cards, selected at random. It depicted a water-colour sketch of an African woman in regal apparel with her nude child comfortably seated on her left arm and supported by her right hand. The boy amused himself with her large necklace, which matched the intricately-carved bracelets on her arms.

Fou-Fou chose to talk about what the mother was wearing and whether or not the boy was cold. Jessica explained about the climate in Africa and pointed to the colour of skin of the woman and her child. Fou-Fou looked at this, put her thumb in her mouth and snuggled under her soft bed-covers. Jessica, on cue, tucked her in.

As she was about to give her a cuddle and a goodnight kiss, Fou-Fou opened her sleepy eyes and, with her thumb still in

41

place, asked, 'Mum, did God paint us?' Jessica was grateful for the distraction the doorbell caused and she retorted something about God using special paint to colour people and flowers and all the things he made as she went to let the baby-minder in.

When she returned to the bedroom, Fou-Fou had already gone to sleep. The baby-minder would be staying overnight. Some of the young girls at Jessica's church could be relied on to baby-sit for her now and then. It was a give-and-take arrangement: Jessica's home, the girls said, provided a peaceful and pleasant change from the routine and domestic pressures in their own homes, and the five pounds was an added bonus.

'I'm glad you could come,' Jessica said as she walked with the girl towards the spare bedroom.

'Yeah, I'm glad too, Jessy. You don't know the bother I have in my house to get out.'

Jessica willed the girl to continue. 'What happened this time?'

'Oh, nothing new. I had to psych myself up to ask Mum; she tells me, "Ask your father." I go to Dad. "What did your mother say?" I tell him she told me to ask you. He then tells me to go and ask Mum because it's up to her. Like an idiot I have to then go and ask her again. When I tell her what me dad says, she says, "Goan then, but just make sure you get to school on time tomorrow." Honestly, it's like they don't believe I'm seventeen and almost eighteen.'

Jessica exhaled audibly as if she was blowing out the last flicker of anger that the girl might have been sustaining. 'Life's like that sometimes, but you'll soon leave that behind. Make yourself comfortable and don't starve yourself. There's plenty of food in the kitchen. Just wash up behind you.'

'Jessica, I hope you don't mind me asking, but me and Bev and Steve was wondering why Mother Walters had to pull you and nobody else to the front like that last night?'

Jessica felt small. She could imagine how she must have become table talk in the homes of some of the brethren. She could feel her body becoming tense. She swallowed and, with a curt 'Wish I knew, love,' put an end to what might have been an interrogation from the young girl. 'I'm going to get ready now,' she continued in her usual amicable tones, and she proceeded to the bathroom, holding her head high. 'After all,' she thought, lapsing into her primary language, 'me an dis pickney no companion.'

Her tall, slender, brown body was reflected back at her from the bathroom mirror tiles. Jessica ran her hands over her naked contour and felt gratified that the diets and exercises that she rigidly followed were worth the effort. The shower of warm, soothing water was revitalizing. She wrapped herself in a towel and went into her bedsit. While she made herself ready she thought about the friends she was going to meet. It was amazing how their lives met and their friendship grew.

Miriam, Cynthia, Claudia, Yvonne and Veronica. Each seemed like God's gift to her, and she attributed their meeting to divine providence rather than blind fate. It felt much more controllable, purposeful and comfortable to express it in this way. Yet the circumstances of their meeting were a muddle.

Miriam and Cynthia were the first to have met, because Miriam's mother and the aunt with whom Cynthia lived had been bosom friends from the time they had arrived in England and shared a bedroom. Jessica recalled Cynthia's booming voice: 'Of all the things my aunt has given me, nothing beats my introduction to serious Christianity.' Jessica shook her head as she remembered Cynthia and her aunt, who both had very strong convictions and were very involved in their church.

Then Claudia had joined the twosome. She had mocked them in the fifth form when she was part of the in-crowd and they had disdained the group and its fondness for boys, discos and make-up. But when she was in the sixth form Claudia had become a Christian and attached herself to them. Their particular brand of Christianity and their obvious academic prowess set them apart from their contemporaries.

Veronica came from the same village in Jamaica where Claudia had been born. She arrived in England fifteen years later to attend university and had renewed contact with her childhood friend. Now she divided her time between the two countries: 'When it gets too hot in Jamaica, I come to England;

43

when it gets too cold in England, I return to Jamaica,' she would say, teasing her listeners with the double meaning.

Finally, there was Yvonne, a new friend that Veronica had made at university. Each in their own way had been a point of reference for Jessica when she had become pregnant and her own family had turned away from her. They had redoubled their support when she decided to move to her present home away from Fou-Fou's father, who had no intention of marrying her. Their lives were truly tangled.

Jessica brought her mind back to the present. She gathered her hair, which was plaited with extensions, into a bundle and clipped it. Then she shook it loose and decided to let it hang wild to go with her safari dress. She gave her mirror image an approving smile and felt pleased that the evening would be one of those occasions when to turn up without a male partner would not be a source of regret. She took her handbag, felt for her keys and went to check on Fou-Fou. Then she called to the young girl and double-checked that all was well before she left to collect Miriam.

Miriam was ready and waiting. Jessica noted that her friend carried herself well, even though her body showed that she had had children, and her hair, though curly permed, was Afro-combed. Her husband, Mark, walked with her to the car. Jessica thought what a supportive husband he was and got out of the car to meet them half way. Mark gave Jessica a hug and said frivolously, 'What conspiracy are you all up to tonight, then?'

'He envies our comradeship,' teased Miriam.

'I don't know about comradeship; it's the conspiracy that concerns me,' Mark rejoined as they walked towards the car.

'He's just miserable because he has to look after the kids tonight while I go and put my feet up with friends,' Miriam confided to Jessica. 'See you later, darling.'

Miriam kissed Mark and got into the car. Mark wished them a good time and waved them goodbye.

Miriam buckled her seat-belt and organized herself just as Jessica expected. She had known Miriam since Sunday School, although they had not been firm friends until they were young women.

'Yvonne told me there'd just be the five of us,' Jessica said as she drove out of Miriam's driveway.

'No male partners,' replied Miriam, 'and of course Cynthia's in Zimbabwe. Did you get a card from her?'

Jessica had no difficulty in recalling Cynthia's card. 'Yes, I have it pinned up in my study and I can see her phrase now: "Black women whose success comes out of the motivation and demands of other black women have to be winners."'

'She must have put that on all her cards, at least to the five of us,' commented Miriam. 'Mark read it and got quite heated. He said quite categorically that that is not the full truth. Well, you can imagine what followed. We had to agree to disagree.'

'I think she's right, and, what's more, I think she's talking from experience.' Jessica had to stop the conversation to concentrate on driving as she braked for a zebra crossing, but then continued.

'About Cynthia's message: I think her life is a continuation of her aunt's own success story.'

'Mm . . . well, I think her success is an achievement of all the members of her church. I could feel that at her farewell meeting. It was all really very moving.' Jessica grunted approvingly and Miriam continued. 'I felt proud of her and proud to be her friend. Well, you understand what I mean, not pride in the sense of . . . ' Miriam cut short her explanation as she sensed Jessica's disapproval of her repeating the obvious.

'Why is it such a problem for us to face up to rightful pride and success?' asked Jessica rhetorically. Then she added, 'I guess the words "success" and "winners" in her message were the considered result of her effort to come to terms with them in her own life.'

'She is so modest,' said Miriam.

'Yes,' Jessica confirmed.

'Remember how she defended her position as an ordinary member of her church at the farewell meeting?' Miriam asked. 'Whatever she thought, her pastor obviously regarded her as an outstanding member of the fellowship. I'm really pleased for

Cynthia. She's done well. I'd love to visit her in Zimbabwe, but with a husband and three children . . . '

'You know Mark wouldn't mind if you went without him. He would look after the children, or your parents would, if you really wanted to go,' Jessica retorted.

This must have jogged Miriam's consciousness of Jessica's difficulty in finding child-minders at the best of times, so the rest of the journey was filled with conversation about the children's growth, the cost of feeding and clothing children and the general circumstances of life — their interests, work, home, love and church. Jessica made sure that not too much was said about church. She wanted the opinion of the four friends collectively. She could always follow it up with Miriam on the way home.

The effort of talking and driving reminded Jessica that it was the evening of a working day. She felt famished and, when they got out of the car, she found herself looking forward to a relaxing armchair and a hot home-cooked meal.

Yvonne was at the door to welcome them. 'The last of the merry band,' she announced as she ushered Jessica and Miriam into her spacious lounge. Claudia and Veronica were each curled up in an armchair, beaming with the bliss of the moment and the anticipated pleasure. Jessica and Miriam completed the scene. Bob Marley's 'One Love' playing quietly in the background reinforced Jessica's awareness that her friends were not confined by the dogmas and restrictions of their common background. Jessica would have loved to have eaten in the comfort of the lounge, but she knew that such informality was not Yvonne's way. She was so unlike Jessica when it came to domesticity.

Jessica had changed to accommodate Fou-Fou, but under other circumstances she loathed the very idea of spending a lot of time cooking what took considerably less time to consume. Yvonne, however, flourished on the niceties of domestic life. Her bedrooms, lounge, dining-room, kitchen and bathroom were a harmonious blend of colour and design. Her meals, Jessica knew, would more than complement her dining-room suite and cutlery. Jessica asked about Yvonne's husband and children and in reply Yvonne explained that Tony had decided to go and play cricket for his club and that the children were fast asleep. She was free to indulge in quiet companionship.

Jessica's gaze took her into the tranquillity of Yvonne's well-kept garden and from the garden back into the softly-lit dining-room with its peaceful décor and then to the painted vase of freshly-cut flowers on the table.

Yvonne's choice of clothes and jewellery was equally tasteful. Her dress sense had been the main reason for her quarrel with the church deacons: her passion for fashionable hair-styles, clothes and jewellery was regarded as deviation from holiness and a stumbling block to would-be Christians and those who were new to faith.

As she thought of Yvonne's departure from the church that she had encouraged Jessica herself to join when she moved into the area four years previously, she could not help thinking aloud: 'Yvonne, you're brave, you know. Girl, you are brave. You showed them.'

Yvonne's reply was not quite what Jessica expected. 'I've gone past that now, Jessy. I don't really think about things like that now, like I've said countless times to other people who ask me how I feel about leaving Clifton Road Church. I sometimes feel hurt that I had to turn my back on my parents and my church who gave me so much support, especially when I was at university. I also feel bad about the young people who saw me as an example and all that. When you leave church, you leave a lot, if you know what I mean. I just knew that if I didn't get out and do my own thing, I'd crack up. But what's right for me isn't necessarily right for everyone. Everybody having avocado?' she inquired, with more than a tinge of persuasion.

Jessica joined in the responsive chorus, which gratified Yvonne, who loved to please.

'At least you haven't left the Lord, Yvonne,' commented Miriam, in her pacifying voice.

'No,' replied Yvonne. 'I've just chosen another way to do business with him.'

While they ate the first course, they brought one another up-to-date on each of their lives since the last time they had met.

Claudia had much to tell about her first term as deputy head; Veronica was still struggling to write her first novel while working as a freelance reporter; Miriam was enjoying her first year as a full-time pastor's wife. They all listened intently as they heard, for the first time, about some of the radical activities Miriam and Mark were encouraging their small congregation to become involved in, attending meetings on black theology and getting involved with the peace movement. They might seem like ripples of activity to an outsider, but such changes could make waves within their denomination.

Yvonne gathered up the dishes and went to the kitchen to get the second course. She returned with fried plantain, roast chicken, split peas, some rice and a variety of salad dishes. She set each dish and bowl down carefully. The food looked delicious and enticing.

'Food is for eating,' exclaimed Veronica, beginning to serve herself some rice.

'Vee, you grabalitious you know. Do you realize we've eaten the first course without saying grace?' Claudia's jovial rebuke restrained Veronica.

'For health, strength and daily food, we praise your name, God.' Yvonne stood and stretched her hands out across the table. 'All right, Claudia?'

'Mm . . . ' muttered Claudia. 'Short, sweet and spicy.'

'Unlike some graces I have listened to which take you across the world and back while the food gets cold,' Jessica remarked.

'But not forgetting Cynthia in Zimbabwe,' Miriam commented, bringing the memory of their friend to the forefront of their thoughts. 'I hope she's made some friends out there.'

Miriam related such news of Cynthia as she had gleaned from her aunt. Talking about Cynthia made them all feel that she was part of their gathering, and they were glad to have remembered her in this way.

While they helped to clear the plates from the table for the third course, Jessica asked for a considered response to her experience the night before. She told them the details, interspersed with her thoughts, questions and vexed feelings. Her story provoked a response from them all. Yvonne said

48

she couldn't believe that people still carried on like that in church; Claudia explained that, in her local church, anyone who felt they had a special message from God had to take it first to the pastor and elders rather than scream it at the congregation; Veronica was quite certain that she would have demanded to be left alone or to have a public explanation from the sister.

'Why didn't you phone Mark or me to talk about it, Jes?' Miriam enquired gently.

But Veronica had more to say and denied Jessica the chance to reply to Miriam. 'Some people carry on to the point of extremity. They think that God's given them special work to do in running the church. Really they just get carried away in the excitement of the worship.'

Claudia then asked Jessica what she intended to do about the whole thing. At that point Jessica was lost for words. She had thought about her feelings and had examined her spiritual state; she had even considered what she might have done, but not what she was going to do. She contemplated her answer as the others waited in silence, then said, 'I don't know.'

'What do you mean "you don't know"?' Claudia asked. 'Surely you will follow it up with the sister or your pastor?'

'You've really lost your fire, girl,' interrupted Yvonne. 'You're well and truly "saved" and the church has got you in its clutches.' Then, thumping the table as if it were a soap-box she declared, 'I told her that if she really wanted to return to church she should make sure that she went prepared to develop as a person in her own right, not a clone.'

Then it was Veronica's turn to take the floor. She had a way of telling jokes to lighten any situation. 'This one is the honest truth. My brother told me it. He was visiting a church the night they were having what they called an "open discussion" — heart to heart. Well, every church has its Sister Walters, and this one woman kept standing up and interrupting the service with irrelevant texts and opinions. The pastor could tell that everyone else disapproved, and he was getting annoyed too, and at last he said in an authoritarian voice, "Sit down, Sister Burns!" She shrieked back at him, "No, I'm standing up." "Sit down, Sister Burns," he bellowed at her. "No," she insisted, "I'm standing up." By this time the man had reached his limit. "All right," he said. "Stand up, Sister Burns." And the silly old girl was so confused she said, "I'm not taking orders from you — I'm sitting down."'

Before they could compose themselves, Veronica was on to another. They wept with laughter at Veronica's collection of stories, ignoring the fundamental significance. 'How about this one?' she continued. 'My father told me. I can't tell it as well as he can, but I have to tell you. It's so funny. No offence, Jess, but it's your story that reminds me of this one.

'My dad must have been about eighteen. He was sitting in church with his friends, only in those days the men and women were not allowed to sit together — they had to sit on opposite sides of the church. The very serious ones would sit at the front or among the older men, and the less committed ones, including him at that time, were at the back. They usually got involved with everything but the sermon, like eyeing up the girls on the other side or in the choir and watching them blush with fear and embarrassment, especially if one of the mothers intercepted those looks. Anyway, on this particular Sunday morning the pastor had invited a popular young preacher to the church as guest speaker. He sat on the platform and he was a cut above most of the young men. His suit, tie and shirt were complemented by his well-polished shoes, the soles of which looked as if they hardly walked on gravel. My dad always made the point here that most of his friends didn't have a suit, and the soles of their shoes were such that they made sure they kept their feet flat on the ground.

'Anyway, the local pastor got up and started to reel off the credentials of the guest speaker, looking pointedly at the young men as he did so. He was clearly proud to show them such a shining example of spiritual achievement. "Yu see, if yu behave yuselves and live good, God will elevate yu and make yu a blessing." Meanwhile the young women, especially those in the choir, sat there listening intently and wondering if they might be the one to be blessed as his bride. My dad could tell that they'd all made special efforts with their appearance that day. They might have been restricted by the black and white uniform, and straightened hair wasn't allowed, but those who had hair to hang under their hats definitely showed it that morning.

'"Bredrin," the pastor continued, "it is now my pleasure to invite our dear brother into the pulpit to . . . "

'"Lord Jesus," one of the mothers bellowed from the middle of church. Then she made her way up the aisle and round the choir and across the front of the church where she shouted, "Sin in the camp!" My dad said "everybody catch them fright. Who sin and who no sin start pray silently, 'cause once that mother started, nothing could go on until the culprit and sin is revealed."'

'Victim, more likely,' inserted Yvonne.

'And sin as perceived by that church,' added Jessica.

'Carry on, Vee,' cried Claudia, 'and don't let us get into an argument now.'

'Well,' continued Veronica, 'my dad says he will never forget that day. The young Rev. stood in the pulpit unmoved. The mother continued to weave her way onto the platform, round the choir, back onto the platform and back round the choir. Everybody from the pastor down just sat quietly. Only the mother's voice and her footsteps could be heard. The young Rev. started to assert his position: "Oh yes, Amen, Ma'am."

'"In the name of Jesus," retorted the mother, "hold your peace. What is hidden will be revealed. Oh yes . . . something wrong . . . you have to confess."

'Then the mother said she was going to sing a verse of a song and by the time she finished she expected to see two people at the altar. She sang the first verse. Nobody moved. She sang the second verse. Nobody moved. Then she said, "Satan tough," and continued with the third verse. One by one the choir members left their choir seats and went to the altar. The mother, not satisfied, then said, "No sermon today, until the pulpit is left clean." At that point the young Rev. left the pulpit and went to the altar. It wasn't very long after that incident, my dad said, that it became apparent that one of the girls was going to have that guest speaker's child.'

'Well, in those days church life was very dramatic, wasn't it?' stated Claudia.

'I tell my father that I couldn't cope with that kind of carry-on. He tells me that it was because of that incident that he decided to become serious about church,' retorted Veronica.

'Yes, but our faith and the life of the church is not about bullying and fear,' Miriam added with her dependable wisdom. 'It's surely about discovering ourselves in Christ and sharing in the joy of being members of his family.' As she said this, she passed round the gâteau. Then she continued, 'That's just the view of church that many people have, whether they've experienced it or just heard about it, and it's one that Mark and I are trying to correct in our local fellowship.'

'Good for you,' Yvonne said. 'The leadership in a church makes all the difference in the way a church is run.'

'Quite honestly,' replied Miriam, 'it's not so much the official leadership as what the people hold to be the source of authority.'

'I think you're absolutely right,' Jessica observed.

'You see, Jessy,' Claudia took the opportunity to counsel, 'you could be helping yourself and your fellowship if you ask the sister who dragged you to the altar to explain herself.'

'But there comes a time, Claudia, when you have to stop and make a personal decision about how far you want to take on an entire church,' Yvonne countered, her voice slightly unsteady with the emotion of it all. 'That's exactly why I couldn't hang around the Clifton Road Church for any longer. I just couldn't take the responsibility and the pressure.'

'You couldn't or you wouldn't?' asked Miriam.

'Both,' replied Yvonne quite decisively. 'I just want a church where I can go when I like and get involved as much or as little as I choose.'

'Isn't that a bit selfish?' Miriam challenged.

'I don't think so,' Veronica butted in. 'I'm like you, Yvonne. I have no ambition to lead a congregation. My ambition is to write from my Christian convictions. I basically want a church where I can go each Sunday to regenerate my spirit. That's why I go to Lady Hill Tabernacle.'

Yvonne laughed. 'My parents say your church harbours all those who wander from holiness — just because the people don't have a problem about going to church hatless or seeing women wearing jewellery or dressed in trousers.'

'I don't know,' Veronica remonstrated. 'In society, one of the most oppressed groups is black women. I suppose we shouldn't expect our experience in the church to be any different.'

'But,' added Jessica, 'the women are one of the most spiritual groups of people . . . '

'Because of our oppression,' concluded Claudia, 'that's why. Regardless of its failings, I'm staying put in the black led church. For me, church is about more than worshipping.'

'Yes, Mark and I believe that there is a need for a black church in this country at this time,' Miriam stated, supporting Claudia's point. 'Where else can a black person stand up in a group of Christians and talk about the victory you had over some brutal foreman, share the agony you are going through with your neighbour or some bureaucracy and feel the supportive strength that comes when someone says "Amen" or "I'm praying for you"?'

Claudia continued, 'And I think the children who attend black churches have a far wider collection of successful black people for role models.'

'I agree with what you are both saying. The black church has the capacity to absorb and soothe the wounds people bring to it, but you have to make a lot of personal sacrifices to gain that kind of reward,' observed Yvonne. 'If you feel you can cope without that double-edged combination of constraint and support, you can go and worship elsewhere.'

'But contribute to the black Christian voice,' Veronica added, imploring Yvonne with her eyes for confirmation.

'That's right,' affirmed Yvonne. 'You see, Miriam, during my time of searching for the right church, you and Mark were still at training college. I did not have the patience to wait for people like you two to come and lead our black churches, nor did I have the will to take on any sort of leadership responsibility for a church, so I opted for a good multi-racial church.'

'They wouldn't have listened to you anyway, Yvonne. Your adornments got in the way,' Veronica reminded her teasingly.

'Well,' Yvonne shrugged her shoulders in resignation, 'as long as there is a good Christian fellowship not too far from where I live, I am quite happy to go along, whether it's black led or white led.'

Miriam had a further contribution to make. 'Don't misunderstand me. All I'm saying is that a local fellowship of black Christians with black leadership has the potential to carry the people a very long way forward. Mark and I have decided to focus all that we do as leaders on our local community of black people.'

'As far as I'm concerned, the authentic Christian voice must speak to and for all people, the treader and the downtrodden, regardless of the background of the speaker. The Kingdom embraces black and white,' argued Veronica.

'I agree with that,' Yvonne said in earnest.

'Fou-Fou asked me a few weeks ago,' Jessica commented, 'why were there only "brown" people, as she calls us, in our church. Now, I never made that kind of observation when I was a child in Sunday School. In fact, I only asked those questions while I was at college when I had to justify and defend my attendance of the Wednesday evening prayer meetings at a local black Pentecostal church.'

'Why did you seek out a black Pentecostal church, then?' Veronica asked.

'I guess I wanted to be with a group of black people and, quite honestly, I felt I needed the support of a prayer group. I tell you, when I managed to go to those meetings and pour out my soul in the company of those mature and strong Christians, the tiredness, loneliness and whatever might have been pulling me apart just seemed to gather like a snowball and roll away.' Jessica closed her eyes and for a moment relived the times.

'A refuge for the soul,' mused Miriam aloud.

'A shelter in a weary land,' offered Claudia, imitating a church elder.

'A balm for the weary,' Jessica said, shaking her head from side to side. 'For me, the testimonies, the worship, the prayers,

54

the songs, the sermons, and especially the warmth of the other members of my church are a source of healing for my spirit and emotions after a hard week. I get angry when someone spoils that, and last Sunday Mother Walters really interfered with my peace. It would have been so different if she had put her arms around me and prayed for or with me, or at least told me what she had on her mind or what she had discovered.'

'So what are you going to do about her, then?' Yvonne asked.

'Yes, what *are* you going to do?' demanded Veronica.

'I'll have to give more thought to it,' Jessica replied. 'I'll let you know what I decide and how it goes.' In the moment of quiet that followed, the reality of her spiritual state became clear to her. She had cultivated the habit of unloading some of her burdens in the fellowship and accepting the love and care the community offered both to her and to Fou-Fou. At the same time, she had also unloaded responsibility for her spiritual growth and experience and left it in the hands of others. It was as if all she had to do was to attend church services and obey. Suddenly she saw that she had become more conditioned than converted.

'Anyone for coffee?' Yvonne enquired as she made her way to the kitchen in anticipation.

Veronica stood up and stretched. 'I've definitely had a bellyful tonight. Good job I don't start work till two tomorrow afternoon.'

Jessica looked at her watch. She felt relieved that her babyminder was staying overnight.

'We could clear the table and wash up over coffee,' suggested Miriam.

As they washed, wiped, and drank their coffee, they chatted and laughed as if the night had no ending. Each was as delighted as the other to be together.

'Some good things must come to an end,' announced Claudia, as if addressing her assembly of schoolchildren.

At that point, everyone returned to the lounge. Each woman searched through her diary to find a date for a reunion in six months' time, and another half-hour was spent explaining and debating and joking about forthcoming events. Had it not been for the commitments of the following day they might have stretched the time to another hour.

The return journey was as pleasant as the drive to Yvonne's home. For Jessica, there seemed little time between saying goodnight to Miriam, speeding home, locking away the car, entering her house and climbing the stairs to Fou-Fou's bedroom.

Jessica looked down at Fou-Fou. She looked a picture of comfort. The even pace of her breathing contrasted with Jessica's sharp, snatched breath. Just then the conflicts in her own life surfaced in her thoughts and made her feel moment-arily envious of Fou-Fou. Parts of the evening's conversation flashed across her mind. She closed her eyes and shook her head. She pondered about how she and Fou-Fou could find their place in the life of the fellowship.

Jessica, she thought, you are going to have to be more than a passive participant in the church . . . black church . . . move-ment. She experimented with the term 'black church move-ment'. She listened to her thoughts and sighed. Her thoughts became audible. 'I never thought about it as a movement.' Her mutterings were interrupted by the phone.

'Who under God's heaven is calling me at this time of the night?' she asked the thin air as she went into her bedroom to answer, half fearing the unknown.

'Is that you, Sister Jessica?' asked the voice at the other end.

'Yes. Who's calling?'

'It's me, Mother Walters, child. I know it's late and you must be tired but,' she spoke with authority, 'I wanted to talk to you right this moment. The Lord tells me you have a part to play in the church, but you are resisting, Sister Jessica.' With that she started to pray. 'Touch her, Lord,' Mother Walters' voice demanded, 'and mould her . . . give her spiritual energy.' While old Mother Walters prayed, Jessica listened.

Well, she thought, to argue with Mother Walters would be to argue with God. Jessica continued to listen to Mother Walters' prayer.

'Your ways are not our ways, Lord. Have your own way. Amen.'

Jessica could say nothing but her own 'Amen', once again allowing herself to be overpowered by a wisdom beyond her grasp.

A Moment to Care
LOREEN LYSEIGHT

Fay Bailey started from her slumber. It was a second or so before she identified the sound of breaking glass. She moved hesitantly from the bed to investigate. The discovery that someone had, yet again, thrown a brick through the bedroom window filled her being with a mixture of fear and discontent. She vaguely hoped that this recent onslaught of vandalism was not a consequence of having a black skin. It wasn't worth reporting to the police this time. After all, what could they do? From past experience, all they would do would be to take statements and personal details, further invading privacy while admitting their inability to apprehend the offender.

Having attended to the damaged window, Fay climbed back into bed. She shivered and drew the covers closely around her. The flimsy cardboard against the broken glass obviously wasn't going to keep the cold air out. It seemed surprising to her that after thirty years in Britain the chill of English winters still struck her with the same intensity and the cold appeared to penetrate to her very bones. A slow smile gradually formed on her face as she remembered how her daughter, Doreen, would refuse to wear a vest as protection against the cold when she was a child. In a tantrum her little fingers would tear at the garment, her features set in concentrated determination while she attempted to remove it.

As she tried to sleep, she found her thoughts returning to the early years in Jamaica at the time Zeki and she had finalized arrangements for their departure to England. Her husband had been christened Ezekiel, but in their sunshine isle you rarely got through school without a friendly rechristening. So 'Zeki' he became to family and friends alike. Some people had not escaped so lightly: one poor lad who was christened 'Fish Face' at school had retained the name into adult life.

Zeki and Fay had made the decision to leave their homeland after only six months of marriage. There was an abundance of advertisements in Kingston, the heart of the Island, which proclaimed untold wealth and fulfilment in England. Thus was their youthful need for adventure kindled. Neither of them had wished to scrimp and scrape for a living in Jamaica. England beckoned, full of promises. After all, were not even the streets in England paved with gold? In their imagination it was likened to the promised land, a kind of heaven on earth.

The church gave them an inspiring send-off. Fay remembered how Pastor Williams, leader of their flock, had preached a farewell sermon. He encouraged them to reach towards future goals and forget the wrongs that had befallen them in the past. As he warmed to his sermon, he paced the platform vigorously. His words were in turn compelling, penetrating and uplifting. The congregation had responded in 'Amens' and 'Hallelujahs' as they too were caught up in empathy with the message of faith being delivered.

'Brothers and Sisters, when sorrows surround you, and the way seems unclear, get down on your knees to Jesus. Let him know your needs; give thanks for his loving care. When all hope has forsaken you "the peace of God which passeth all understanding shall keep your hearts and minds from faltering."

'Brother and Sister Bailey: you're going to a new country . . . a fresh beginning. Who knows what lies before you? Who knows what will befall you? But remember, in whatsoever state you find yourself, learn to live with it, be content. Know how to bear humiliation. Christ Jesus suffered and — Hallelujah! — he withstood the test. Brother Zeki, sometimes your cup will be full, sometimes you will have no money, no food. But don't think God has deserted you. Just remember that "you can do all things through Christ" who will be your strength. I know that God will supply all of your needs according to his riches in glory. My brethren: I implore you, keep the faith.'

At the end of the sermon, their pastor stood with them at the altar while the brethren filed by, offering a handshake or a hug, kissing with much emotion while the tears rolled unheeded down their faces. There were many admonitions: 'Be good now,' 'Don't forget to write,' 'We're going to miss you both,' and one especially for Zeki: 'Don't stop playing the saxophone for the Lord, it's been a blessing to us.' Most of all, they were bidden keep the faith, come what may.

Old Mother Clarke revelled in praises to God as she clasped them individually to her ample bosom. The large embroidered straw hat, precariously perched on her head, defied gravity as a spontaneous 'Hallelujah' took her by surprise and her body moved rhythmically under the joyous influence of the Holy Spirit.

So sharp was the memory that Fay could recapture the tropical scene almost perfectly: the warm night air and the image of the brethren singing with intensity. Tears welled up in her eyes as she returned in spirit and tried to remember the words to the tune now entering her mind:

> *Till we me-e-eet, till we me-e-eet,*
> *Till we meet at Jesus' feet,*
> *Till we me-e-eet, till we me-e-eet,*
> *God be with you till we meet again.*

An air of finality pervaded the congregation. The embarkation of their beloved sister and brother on a new life in a foreign land gave no assurance of any return to the old one. The occasion gave a strong sense of togetherness in the present and left no space for the possibility of a future reunion this side of heaven.

After the service Mother Clarke had pressed upon them a basket laden with green bananas, yam, mangoes, spicy fried fish and hard-dough bread, as well as coconut drops for a sweet tooth. It was quite possible to believe that England would be in the throes of a food shortage on their arrival. As she embraced them in a final parting, her words to them were 'May God richly bless you both.' Long after the event, Zeki and Fay had found amusement in speculating whether she had meant them to be blessed spiritually or materially.

In contrast, the memory of their arrival and reception in England stood starkly cold. It was a difficult time, those initial years. She remembered how they yearned to be accepted as people in their own right and to be recognized other than by the colour of their skin. The hardship of living in England benumbed them; it was worse than any previous experience of being underprivileged. The irony was that Jamaica now came to represent the haven they had left in search of.

Fay yawned and stretched. She missed the warmth of Zeki's body in the bed. His job as a bus driver entailed shiftwork. Tonight, more than ever, she longed for his comforting presence. Then the shroud of sleep enveloped her, blissfully easing the longing.

Opening her eyes as a creaking sound disturbed her, Fay noticed that Zeki was coming into the bedroom with a tray bearing a cup of tea and the morning paper.

'Hello luv, are you tired?' she asked with concern.

'No, me not so tired,' Zeki replied. 'It make a difference when you don't get any of those hooligans on the shift — you don't feel so anxious. Anyhow, I see they break the windows again. If it carry on like this we may have to think seriously about moving. You can't depend on the police. They think black people invented crime . . . or that crime is only black against white. Sometimes I want to ask both them and the media what so many white people are doing in prison if it's only black people commit crime.' Zeki's voice had risen in anger.

'Don't bother get yourself worked up over them things this time of morning, Zeki. I've put a piece of cardboard over the window for the present. You'll have to mend it soon, though: the weather is too cold to leave it like that for long. Come, rest yourself now,' Fay concluded, picking up the newspaper.

As she finished reading an article in the *Express*, Fay noticed that Zeki had fallen asleep. Carefully easing herself from the warm bedding, she got up to wash and dress.

Saturdays were always a busy time for her. Dressing hurriedly in the bathroom, she now wished she had left reading the paper until later. The bathroom wall, with its mirrored tiling, volunteered her reflection: a tallish figure, dark of skin and attractive, met her gaze. She wore her hair plaited in cane-rows to form a bun at the nape of her neck; it gave her features a slightly austere look. Fay felt grateful that her face was not prematurely lined. After all, life hadn't been one of respite.

As she moved towards the kitchen, the sight of the dark interior of her daughter's bedroom glimpsed through the semi-closed door sent a charge of irritation through her body. Although it was only 8.15 in the morning,

64

the urge to disturb her daughter's calm repose assailed her.

'Doreen, Doreen,' she called sharply. 'You not getting out of bed this morning? You know I'm going to the market. Get up and help to do something.'

The words of her request eluded Doreen as her desire to sleep blocked out the querulous sound of her mother's voice.

'I hope you're listening to me,' Fay continued. 'I'll leave the shopping at Sister Taylor's house. You can collect it from there. Make sure your father has something to eat when he wakes up. I'll get some fish; you can cook that for dinner. I have to visit Sister Davis in the hospital. Tell your father I won't be back till this evening. I have to help out at the church preparing the programme for the Easter weekend services.'

'OK, Mum,' Doreen acknowledged drowsily. The slamming of the front door signalled her mother's departure. Doreen slowly drifted into a fitful sleep and eventually she began to dream that she was putting the shopping away in the kitchen. As she bent to open a cupboard door, reality replaced the dream and she almost toppled out of bed. The glowing figures on the digital clock showed 12.30.

'Mum will kill me,' she muttered as the combination of realizing what time it was and finding that she was still in bed reminded her of chores untended. If only she had inherited some measure of her mother's disciplined approach to life. We're so different, she commented to herself wryly.

Doreen wondered what the church brethren found so appealing in her mother. They presented her with even the simplest of problems and 'Sister Bailey' obviously relished her role of problem-solver. Doreen couldn't imagine discussing her personal difficulties with her mother — there was no hope of being understood. The woman was unapproachable even when they weren't clashing. Stolid! That's the word for her! She summed up her thoughts drily.

Doreen dressed, aware of the passing minutes but somehow unable to make her limbs move any faster. Mum's faithful friend was sure to rebuke her, however mildly, for not coming earlier.

The journey to Sister Taylor's house normally took around twenty minutes. Today the bus crawled along in the heavy traffic. Doreen felt a sense of annoyance beginning to overwhelm her. Acutely conscious of the time, she raised her watch-hand constantly to her gaze. The bus reached her stop; she got off with a sigh of relief and raced down the side street to Sister Taylor's three-storeyed house. Panting heavily, she rang the doorbell.

The door opened. 'Girl, you late you know,' Sister Taylor greeted her. 'It's no wonder you mother get cross with you sometimes.' Then, ushering Doreen into the kitchen, she asked, 'You want a cup of tea?'

'No thanks,' Doreen responded curtly.

'You must help your mother, child, you shouldn't wait for her to ask you. Tell me — what you have to do with yourself? You not working. You mother and father go to work, life not easy for them, you know.'

'Can I have the shopping please, Sister Taylor? I'm in a hurry,' Doreen said, trying to contain her anger. The last thing she needed now was a lecture.

'Oh, so you know how to hurry now! I've been waiting all morning for you. You didn't know you could hurry then, eeh?' replied Sister Taylor as she handed over the groceries. The two women made their way towards the front door.

'When you coming to church?' she continued. 'We haven't seen you for quite some time. Remember, the world doesn't have anything to offer you. If it's success you're seeking, Jesus will lead you there.'

'Well, you may see me soon,' Doreen replied politely. 'Bye, Sister Taylor.'

She felt acutely embarrassed as she left the house. She loathed the idea that she might have been a topic of concern between Sister Taylor and her mother.

When she arrived home, Doreen ascertained that her father was still asleep and then went to the kitchen. She liked her dad, although she felt he was a mis-match for her mother. She couldn't understand how someone so even-tempered could have fallen in love with as demanding a figure as her mother, let alone marry her. He wasn't bad looking, considering his age. His smooth brown skin and soft curly hair suggested a modicum of Indian or white ancestry, but his nose testified firmly to his black roots. His keen sense of humour made him much more approachable than her mother, and the easy banter that flowed between them inspired no such amusement in her mother.

Doreen mused on her mother and their conflicting relationship. They had nothing in common. Where did one begin when there wasn't common ground for communication? Maybe there was something though, she thought sardonically: arguments!

Looking round the kitchen, she felt pleased that she had accomplished the chores so quickly. It was time to do some studying now. She had her mock exams soon. The fish could wait until later; it wouldn't take long to cook.

In her bedroom, Doreen lost all sense of time as she concentrated on her revision. Eventually, she raised her head as she lay prostrate among the textbooks and notes that surrounded her. A sound that had been nagging at her mind gained dominance over her studious involvement. Listening intently, Doreen tried to identify it. She frowned as she made an effort to recollect who else was in the house. Suddenly, the stamping sound of feet marching purposefully upstairs issued its own warning of impending unpleasantness. The realization that her mother had returned had barely registered when the bedroom door flew open.

'Do — reen!' Her mother's voice thundered and reverberated in the small space. Her eyes scanned the untidy bedroom, taking in the chaos of books littering the floor, the crumpled bed and the items of clothing piled haphazardly over the chair. The unused ironing-board standing in the corner made its own statement.

'Yes, Mum,' she answered, blushing. Doreen heard her voice squeak; it was not firm and strong as she had intended. She was twenty-one years old, but Mum treated her more like twelve. She had meant to hang the clothes up, but the time had really flown. There wasn't any need for her mother to verbalize her thoughts. The unrelenting stare by now had Doreen squirming where she lay.

Looking up awkwardly from the floor, she strained to contain her mother's penetrating stare. At this angle, the woman seemed taller and even more threatening than usual. Lying on the floor in this kind of situation was certainly a disadvantage. She wondered whether to get up, but her body seemed glued to the floor. The problem was that her neck was beginning to ache. As Doreen moved her head to relieve the stiffness, her mother yelled, 'Look at me when I'm speaking to you! Haven't you got any manners?'

'Yes, Mum.' Doreen's voice was almost inaudible.

'Don't yes Mum me. So what happen? You think you're too good to go in the kitchen. If you know how much your father and I suffer, working all the hours God sends, just so that you can have a good education and decent clothes to wear. You want the best of everything and you can't even cook one little piece of fish! You're an ungrateful little wretch,' Fay shouted. Then she continued in a quieter voice: 'Look at my clothes.'

Doreen looked. She couldn't see anything wrong with her mother's clothes. Dressing well was her mother's most apparent vanity.

'You have the best,' her mother said bitterly, 'while your father and I walk around in rags . . . rags I tell you.' Fay's voice had now risen alarmingly. 'How could you lie around up here, doing nothing, with the kitchen in such a state? You're a girl-child and should know better than that.'

'Mum, I tidied the kitchen. I was going to go back down but I forgot the time. I've got my exams at Easter . . . '

'All you think about is books,' Fay interrupted. 'You don't fool me with those books: they're just an excuse not to do anything in the house. You can fool your father with those books but not me, my dear! When you do make a move, eating and sleeping is all you care about. Well, let me tell you, we're not running a hotel or a holiday camp.'

'But I . . . I . . . I . . . ' Doreen stammered as she tried to explain. It seemed almost impossible to proffer an explanation amid her mother's torrent of words. Closing her lips firmly against further endeavours to reply only provided a signal to launch her mother afresh.

'So you don't have a mouth. Isn't it you I'm talking to?'

Gritting her teeth, Doreen fought to withhold the tears of anger and frustration that threatened to flood her eyes. Her self-control was being systematically eroded. Fay, noting her daughter's undoubted distress, left the room abruptly. 'May God give me grace,' she grumbled.

Zeki, who had been listening to this outburst from the bedroom, joined Fay in the living-room.

'Fay, I know you mean well, but don't you think you're a bit hard on Doreen sometimes? Remember, she's growing up in a different age to us. We learnt to fend for ourselves and handle money carefully because we had to, what with having to send a portion of our wages back home to keep our folks off the breadline and things like that. After all, when you really think about it, we took on the work because we didn't want our children to suffer the way we did.'

'You were always too soft on her,' Fay responded.

'No, hear me out, Fay. What I'm trying to say is the fact that we've made sacrifices to benefit them has little or no meaning to her. OK, the older ones have left home now, but they too had this attitude that we owed them the best in life. Now Doreen thinks we can offer her the world.'

'Listen to me, Zeki. Doreen needs to learn that life is not just about receiving. I know the saying "it's far better to give than to receive", but that doesn't mean there's only going to be a giver. Someone has to receive, but I don't see why it should be one way.'

'I wasn't trying to make excuses for her, Fay. All I'm saying is that we tried to give them the things we didn't have, like time to study, so that they wouldn't have to struggle. We can only do so much to make Doreen appreciate things from our point of view. If you're too heavy-handed and don't try to understand her thinking, it will only serve to drive a wedge between her and us.'

'Well, all I know is that if it wasn't for me she wouldn't

amount to anything. Doreen needs to be pushed before she'll do anything for herself, let alone for anyone else,' Fay said, curtailing the discussion. 'I'm going into the kitchen to prepare something to eat, which I wouldn't have to do if Doreen had been the least bit helpful.'

An hour later Fay commenced laying the table for the meal. She resolved not to call Doreen for her dinner; she could stay in the bedroom sulking if she so desired.

The mackerel, served with flour dumplings, boiled carrots and peas, looked extremely appetizing and smelt equally so. As Zeki sat down he remarked, 'Isn't Doreen eating now?'

'She knows where the kitchen is. She can't expect people to wait on her hand and foot,' Fay replied testily.

Later on, after Zeki had left for work, Fay settled herself on the sofa. She would study the Sunday School lesson before she tackled some ironing. She looked at the Bible text that illustrated the theme for the lesson: ' . . . he that loveth not his brother whom he hath seen, how can he love God whom he hath not seen?' Her conscience was pricked. The Bible verse seemed almost condemning when viewed in the context of her relationship with Doreen. The thought was quickly suppressed. She didn't wish to dwell on the lack of warmth between herself and her daughter. Besides, Zeki's words still rankled somewhat. Doreen could be heard moving around upstairs, and the heavy beat of the music from her stereo finally broke Fay's concentration.

Fay decided to start the ironing instead. On her way to set up the ironing-board, Fay switched on the television. She felt that she got on much better with the ironing when she wasn't concentrating totally on it. Watching the television or listening to the radio somehow helped to take her mind off the manual activity and made it seem less of a chore. After watching the news and weather report, she switched off and turned on the radio. Suddenly, a vague feeling that she was not alone made her turn to see Doreen edging into the room.

'Doreen, how many times do I have to ask you not to creep

around like that?' Fay asked in annoyance. She noticed that Doreen seemed to be dressed for a night on the town. Her slender figure was encased in a figure-hugging black dress. Her hair was worn in a fashionable straight bob. She exuded a youthful glow and her delicate make-up emphasized her cool complexion.

'What time is it?' Fay asked quite deliberately.

'Ten-thirty,' Doreen replied stoically.

'Ten-thirty at night, Doreen, is when people plan to go to bed, not when they decide to go out.'

'Mum, I already told you last week that Barbara invited me to her party,' explained Doreen patiently.

'Party?' Fay looked at her daughter in disbelief. 'What kind of party start so late at night . . . eeh . . . you tell me that now?'

'It's her twenty-first birthday,' Doreen snapped back as the tension rose within her. The woman just had to spoil everything. Just because she didn't believe in having fun, she had to prevent everyone else from enjoying life. The original elation of anticipating a good night out was fast subsiding.

'So, what happen to your studies? It's not important now?' Fay queried.

'I haven't been anywhere for ages, Mum. It is her twenty-first. You're only twenty-one once,' Doreen replied angrily.

'Oh, so your studies are only meaningful when I need you to help out?'

Doreen felt annoyed that she had allowed herself to become involved in this kind of conversation when she was about to go out. Mum certainly chose her moments!

'What is it with you, Mum? When I was younger, you made me study even when I didn't want to. OK, so I didn't appreciate it then; but now I see the point. And now you say I'm only playing around with books. The first chance I have for a little relaxation you have to argue about it. What am I supposed to do? I can't live my life through you.'

The words shook Fay, but she hid the emotion well. 'So who's asking you to live my life? Don't come to me with your high-falutin ideas. I know what you're implying. I tried to help you by suggesting nursing as a career. Now you want to throw it in my face.'

Oh no, not now, Doreen thought. They had been through all this before. Never mind the fact that she hadn't the slightest inclination to be a nurse. Her mother was still rambling on, and Doreen silently mimicked the familiar words being repeated by her mother. 'The world will always need a nurse; back home everyone respected nurses. At least you know there'll be a job no matter where in the world you travel. They're crying out for nurses everywhere.'

As Fay finished, Doreen took up the argument in spite of herself. 'Don't forget to mention that black nurses almost never get promotion to better-paid jobs in the Health Service. What's more, from what I can see quite a few of them have to do extra work on the agency to earn a decent living. And as for respect, black nurses perform some of the most soul-destroying jobs in the hospital. Do you really think they're respected, or for that matter appreciated? Maybe that's what you had in mind for me,' Doreen ended sarcastically.

'You know your trouble, child? Those books turn your head. Go on, go to your party! You'll get what you don't want, just wait and see. Why can't you be more like your cousin, Jackie? Your Aunt May never had these kind of problems with her. Look at her now . . . passed her diploma in education and she's teaching now. Besides, she didn't let education keep her away from God. You talk about soul destroying: what about your soul and God? Have you given any thought to that? Tomorrow is Sunday, a day of worship. The Good Book says, "Render unto Caesar the things that are Caesar's and unto God the things that are God's."'

In the background, the radio broadcaster ended the news summary. This was followed by the signature tune of one of Fay's favourite radio programmes. The announcer's introduction took precedence over Fay's discourse. 'Are you depressed, insecure, dissatisfied? We want to bring to you a message of hope . . . ' the voice from the radio entreated. Mercifully, the doorbell rang at this juncture, heralding the arrival of Ricky, Doreen's escort to the party.

Addressing her mother, Doreen said, 'I'm not going to argue with you now, Mum. You're just doing your best to upset me and prevent me from going out, but it's not going to work. Why don't you listen to your programme? Maybe it will solve your problems so you can let the rest of us get on with our lives.' Doreen made a quick exit from the room as the doorbell continued to ring insistently.

A minute or so later, Fay heard the front door slam shut. She dwelt on the audacity of the girl. For a while now Fay had felt severe doubts concerning the value of her Christian faith in her relationship with Doreen. The sound judgment she used in other areas of her life seemed to elude her in altercations with her daughter. It probably had something to do with the nearness of those close to you . . . made it harder to be objective . . . allowed your emotions to rule your head.

The Christian concept of being charitable to those who ill-treated you, she felt, enabled her to deal with confrontation with strangers or people who were less well known to her. Her thoughts went back a few weeks to the incident in the corner store near her workplace. She had gone in to buy some coffee for a colleague. The assistant who took Fay's money had studiously ignored the hand Fay opened to receive her change. Instead, she had placed the money on the counter. It was almost as though she thought she might catch a fatal disease if she came into contact with Fay's black hand. Fay felt hurt and humiliated at this uncalled-for attitude.

'Lady, my hand is waiting for the change,' she had said. 'I know that in your ignorance you feel quite pompous about touching my black hand. However, you willingly took payment from the same hand and it certainly didn't harm you, so I would be grateful if you would return my change the same way.' The assistant had been red with embarrassment, although not at all sorry. The predominantly white queue behind Fay had shuffled uncomfortably, knowing the deed was wrong yet prepared to defend one of their own. Fay heard someone mutter in the background that 'some people had jobs to go to,' and she had left the shop in anger. She determined not to spend another penny in that shop, but later, when she considered the Christian commitment to being kind to one's enemies, she had changed that resolution.

By contrast, in her dealings with Doreen the right words seemed to evade her. It hadn't always been like this. It was when she was around thirteen years of age that Doreen's attitude had become quite belligerent. Animosity replaced the cosy harmony that had previously existed between them. Fay had refused to submit to or be thwarted by a defiant child. Instead of seeking understanding and compromise, each had sought to impose her will on the other, and so the foundation for the present discord was laid.

Placing the iron on its rest, Fay felt so weary and depressed that she found herself pleading to God in prayer right where she stood. Tears stung her eyes as she cried out to God: 'Lord, release me from this burden; I've done my best, but I'm only human and apt to fail. Give me strength and courage to resolve this estrangement, for I know it's against your will. I put my trust in you, for I know your word says "I can do all things through Christ" who, praise God, will give me strength. Dear Lord, of myself, I know not what to do but by your grace I believe this situation can be changed . . . Amen!'

A certain calmness came over her, perhaps in part a relief at finally admitting that there was a problem she was unable to resolve alone. Pride, she felt, was the heaviest cross she had to bear. There were many, she knew, who held her in deference and regarded her as a spiritual example in her church. The fear of appearing anything less prevented her from displaying her real emotions or being open about negative areas in her life. Fay abhorred the idea of airing her private failings for public examination. The fact that people came to her for counselling and guidance and, in so doing, had to expose their own imperfections did little to encourage her to reciprocate. She realized that when others had shared with her their own private sorrows this had led to a greater closeness and understanding. Yet even this knowledge had not freed her to share her personal worries with others. She felt a sudden deep respect for those who had overcome their failings in order to attain a better quality of life.

74

Fay suddenly felt desperate to talk to someone about how she was feeling. She thought of her close friend and church sister, Inez Favell. They had met years ago when their families shared the same house during the early days in England. Inez knew more about her than any other acquaintance. If anyone could penetrate the façade she had built around herself, then Inez was the one. The first step towards achieving her goal would be taken if she could bring herself to confide in someone. She sat on the sofa, picked up the phone and cradled it in her arms. Poignant memories of all those times that she and Inez had shared brought a further influx of tears, and an urgent need for human contact impelled her fingers to dial. Inez sometimes had a tendency to ramble on once she got talking, but she was, at the same time, consoling.

'Hello.' The gentle rise and fall of Inez's voice came over the telephone line.

'Inez . . . it's Fay . . . how are you?' Fay replied at long last, her voice choked with emotion.

'Fay Bailey, you know God will bless you. My mind just this moment ran on you.' The silence at the other end of the line was poignant. Inez carried on talking in a bid to break the uneasy tension. 'Do you know, I was just thinking how we overcame all those pressures we were under when we first arrived in England. So many things that could have discouraged us, but the Lord certainly kept us through those times. I don't know what might have become of us. I daily thank God for your friendship and the support the brethren gave us then, even when they too were feeling the pinch. So tell me, Fay, what's wrong?'

Inez hadn't changed. Fay felt more positive as she listened, and Inez's speech had given Fay time to bring her emotions under control.

'To tell the truth, Inez, I was just thinking about those times too, among other things. That's why I'm calling you. Something's been bothering me, and I feel I can confide in you.' She paused. 'I don't know if you realized, but Doreen and myself seem to have been in conflict for some while now.'

There! She had admitted it.

'Every parent go through that, you know, love. Don't get disheartened,' replied Inez's sweet voice.

Fay felt the need to explain. 'No, no, no, Inez. This is more than what we all expect to go through. When I think of the animosity that stands between myself and Doreen, I feel that I've failed in my Christian duty. I've tried to reason with her, but things are getting worse instead of improving.'

'I'm sorry,' Inez said uncomfortably, now somewhat at a loss.

Fay continued. 'Tonight I was looking at the Sunday School lesson and the scripture which says that "he that loveth not his brother whom he hath seen, how can he love God whom he hath not seen", and it set me wondering about how I actually live out my Christian values.'

'My dear Fay, I didn't realize things were like that. I know Doreen is a bit cheeky sometimes, but so are my own children and a host of young people today. Then why you never mention this before? Are you really saying that you've lost the love you felt for her?'

'Not exactly.' Fay hesitated. 'It's more that I find it difficult to express it. When you know that your daughter only sees you as some sort of prim and proper figure, it's very galling. Have you ever tried to show affection to someone you know doesn't respect you?' Fay sighed. 'Maybe if Doreen had made a regular commitment to God, things might have been different. Inez, how is it that your children can worship the Lord and none of mine are interested? What have I done wrong? I took them to Sunday School from the time they were babies!' Fay felt even more distressed.

'You mustn't think like that,' said Inez soothingly. 'You did your best. "You can lead a horse to water but you can't make it drink." But there must be a way you can show her you're doing things for her benefit. She's a sensible child: if you talk to her she might understand.'

'With Doreen, no matter what you do or say, she'll find a way to make it into an argument,' Fay muttered angrily. She felt that Inez had totally underestimated the problem.

'Anyway, how long all this been going on? I remember there was a time when she wouldn't leave your side.'

'She was in her early teens,' Fay recalled. 'I tell you, puberty has a lot to answer for. Once Doreen reached that stage, she decided she was an adult. She had a face on her that would frighten Godzilla. She was morose and unpredictable and you couldn't tell her anything. She knew it all. It seemed like over-night I was dealing with someone else's child. Inez, even the thought of it depresses me.'

'Perhaps you should allow her a measure of independence. I remember the problems I had with Pauline. The best I could do at the time was to try to listen to her without over-reacting. It wasn't easy. The way she spoke to me sometimes was so insulting . . . I would never have dared to speak to my mother like that! Brother Favell and I talked it over one night, and he reminded me how strict our parents were and how we strained to get off the leash when we weren't allowed to speak our minds. We didn't like the way they treated us then. When I looked at our situation with Pauline, I began to see how defiant and cheeky we must have appeared to our parents, especially in those days. It made me try to see things from Pauline's point of view.'

'I don't quite see what you're getting at, Inez.'

'OK. To begin with, every time Pauline displayed her new-found eloquence, I wanted to inform her that I was the mother, not vice versa; but I kept my peace. Even when my tongue was bouncing around in my mouth to say something to put her in her place, God gave me grace to be silent. So you see, you're not alone.'

'Inez, you all get on so well! Your whole family seems to relate so easily, to me as well. I'd no idea.'

'Well, I hope what I've said will help you. Sometimes when you know that others have walked the same path, you feel less alone. When all seems to be failing we have our dear Lord to turn to anytime we need to. Tell him all your wor-ries and a ray of light comes shining through in the darkest terrain.'

Fay felt a sudden sense of relief. 'I'm so glad I called you.

77

It's been a help just talking it over with someone outside the family.'

'If you want to talk further we can arrange to meet soon. Don't bottle up your problems, sister, it's not worth it. That is why so many of our people are being consigned to the mental homes. They kept their troubles to themselves. Perhaps they had no choice: there are not many people around these days who'll take the time to share their brother's struggle, not like the old days. We're all caught up in the race for success. Yes, Christians too. Not that I've got anything against ambition, but merely that sometimes we lose the human touch in this aggressive world. Everyone's in a hurry, no time to stop and help a friend in need, no time to stop and do a thankful deed.' Inez finally ran out of steam.

'Thanks for listening, Inez, but most of all for understanding. I'd better get off this line now. Zeki will have a fit when he sees the phone bill. He already claims that when Doreen gets on the phone we need a second mortgage to cover the cost. You'll hear from me soon. I'll make time to have a talk with Doreen. By the time we see each other again, by the grace of God, I'll have this problem buried. Praise him! I feel better already.'

'Well, Fay, if you need me just remember I'm always here. Bye for now and God bless you!'

Fay felt more at ease as she replaced the handset. She had taken another step forward. The warmth and understanding Inez had shown brought about a certain satisfaction within her. It was so good to have a caring friend.

She started to put the ironing away. A casual glance at the time showed the lateness of the hour. How typical of Inez not to chide her for ringing so late. She decided to get ready for bed and resolved not to wait up for Doreen, for a change.

Ricky and Doreen left Barbara's party in a state of elation. Ricky automatically turned the car in the direction of Doreen's home, and Doreen was so busy chattering that it wasn't until they were a street away from her house that she realized where they were. The familiar signs jolted Doreen's memory into a vivid image of her departure that evening.

'Ricky, stop the car!' she commanded.

'Why?'

'Just do as I say. Stop the car.'

Ricky pulled over to the kerb. 'What's the matter, Doreen? Is there something wrong? Or were you thinking of attacking me?' He laughed at this last remark.

'Don't be stupid,' Doreen replied, laughing with him. 'It's just that Mum and I argued before I came out. I can't face another argument beginning "What time do you call this?" One thing leads to another, and before you know it, you've lost sight of what started the quarrel in the first place.'

'What do you want to do?' asked Ricky. 'I can't really invite you to my place. Mum would freak out, especially as I haven't asked her first.'

Doreen had her own ideas on where she would spend the night, but nevertheless she was disappointed that Ricky hadn't been more helpful. In fact, she was sure there had been an edge of panic in his voice. 'It's all right, Ricky, you don't have to worry that I'm going to land myself on you. Take me round to Debbie's — I know she'll put me up.'

'Doreen, do you know what time it is? Nearly 3.30! Are you sure she'll be awake?'

'She's always up late even though she has Steven. I don't know where she finds the energy sometimes. I babysit for her now and again. Steven's really bright for a five-year-old. He can do a lot for himself, but I get worn out after one evening with him.'

'Debbie lives on that estate behind Highfields Park, doesn't she?'

Doreen nodded in affirmation. Ricky started the car and set out for Debbie's flat. 'I haven't seen her for ages,' he continued. 'Is she still living with that guy, what's his name . . . Patrick? I never liked him. He always seemed a bit peculiar to me.'

'No, he got some other girl pregnant and then moved in with her. I don't think he bothers to give Debbie any money for Steven. I can't understand how she didn't suspect that he was seeing someone else. Mind you, he was lying to her, telling her he was working shifts when all the time he was at the other girl's flat.'

Ricky frowned. 'I just can't believe how some guys act. She's well shot of him. From what I've heard, that guy is bad news!'

Doreen nodded in agreement. 'I think she's better off without him. She's gone back to college part-time. But she's still unhappy about him. I think she's secretly hoping that he'll come back to her.'

'By the way, Doreen, are you going to let your mother know where you are?'

'What for? It's only one night and anyway I'll be home tomorrow.' By this time they had arrived on the estate. 'You can stop here, it's the end of the block,' instructed Doreen. Ricky brought the car to a halt. He got out of the car with Doreen.

'I'll come up with you, make sure she's in. You don't want to be stranded at this hour,' he said.

As he climbed the stairs to Debbie's third-floor flat, the stench of urine on the unwashed stairs was unmistakable. 'Good grief, it really stinks,' Ricky remarked. 'I just don't know how people can do such things in lifts and places like this. I mean, it's their home, man!'

'I know what you mean,' Doreen replied, wrinkling her nose in distaste. 'Debbie can't stand it. Her measures are really drastic. She mops her bit of stairs with neat disinfectant. The smell of that knocks you for six before you even get to the door.' They laughed in unison as they reached Debbie's front door. 'Here we are. Look, the light's on. She must be up,' Doreen said as she pressed the doorbell.

'Who is it?' Debbie's throaty voice called out.

'It's only me — Doreen. I was wondering if you would let me stay the night.'

Debbie opened the door to let Doreen in. As she saw Ricky in the semi-darkness she asked in an overly-bright voice, 'Hi, stranger. You coming in?'

'No, I just dropped Doreen off. I'll see you all later.'

Doreen closed the front door and followed Debbie into the

lounge. There was something peculiar about the room. As she looked round it dawned on her what it was.

Uncharacteristically, the room was in a mess. The coffee table seemed overloaded with used glasses; one glass still contained some drink. An uncapped brandy bottle, almost empty, stood beside the glass. The ashtray was so full that bits of ash had escaped and lay scattered on the glass-topped table. Debbie settled herself in the large sofa and stared fixedly at the television.

'Debbie, what's all this, man?'

'Video! I get them in when I can't sleep.'

'I'm not talking about the video. Look at this room. And your eyes are so red, you look like you've been crying. I've never seen you like this.'

'Oh, lay off, Doreen. Give a girl a bit of peace.'

'Since when have you started smoking?' Doreen persisted.

'Listen, Doreen, I know you mean well, but I don't feel like talking at present. You can have my bedroom — I mostly sleep on the sofa nowadays. I promise you we'll talk in the morning. You're giving me a headache with all your questions.'

Vaguely disturbed, Doreen got ready for bed. The small amount of alcohol consumed at the party plus her physical weariness made it impossible for her to make the connection she sought. Before long she was asleep.

It seemed as though only five minutes had passed before she was being prodded into wakefulness.

'Auntie Doreen, Auntie Doreen,' the urgent cries gradually reached her consciousness. Doreen opened her eyes to see Steven desperately trying to wake her. His little face was tearstained and he looked pleadingly towards her.

'What is it, Steven? Are you hungry?'

He shook his head. 'It's Mummy, she's not well . . . she won't wake up.'

'It's all right, Steven. She's just fast asleep. She went to bed very late, you know.' Doreen spoke reassuringly.

'No!' he screamed, and his hands continued to tug at her.

'All right, Steven, don't cry, I'm getting up.' She was sorry

81

now that she hadn't gone home the previous night. At least she would have been left to sleep in peace.

Entering the lounge with Steven trailing behind her, she called out to Debbie. There was no response. Doreen shook her violently in a bid to obtain some kind of reaction. She wanted to slap Debbie, but with Steven screaming tearfully in the background decided against it.

Suddenly fearful, she held her hand beneath Debbie's nostrils and was relieved to find her still breathing. 'Thank God she's alive,' she murmured to herself.

Television programmes containing scenes like this flashed through her mind as she considered the best course of action. She wasn't even sure what was wrong with her friend. Bits of knowledge came to her . . . keep the person moving . . . don't let them . . . was it don't let them sleep? Doreen felt quite helpless. She couldn't deal with this on her own. Perhaps she should call an ambulance. But then again, if Debbie had taken anything other than alcohol, people might start interfering with Steven. She couldn't allow him to be taken into care.

As panic rose up within her, she decided to call her mother. Her fingers were trembling so badly that she could barely control them to key in the right numbers. It seemed like a lifetime before anyone answered.

'Mum, Mum!' Doreen called frantically.

'What's the matter, Doreen? Where are you?' Fay asked, instantly alert despite the fact that she had been sleeping. 'Doreen, answer me: have you had an accident?' Her heart gave a lurch as this thought hit her.

'No, Mum.' She began weeping with relief now that there was someone to talk to, and she could barely get the words out to explain. 'I spent the night at Debbie's. She won't wake up, Mum. Steven won't stop crying. I don't know what to do.' Her voice was almost breaking.

'Doreen, listen to me,' Fay said forcefully. 'Calm yourself . . . I'll drive over. Debbie: is she the one who lives near the park?' As Doreen confirmed this, Fay continued: 'Just try to keep calm and I'll get there as soon as I can. By the way, have you called an ambulance?'

'No, I wasn't sure whether she was ill because she'd been drinking or because of something else. I was really thinking of Steven . . . I just don't want him to be taken into care.'

'OK, Doreen, just try to keep her body moving and don't let her sleep too heavily. I won't be too long.'

Waiting for her mother's arrival, Doreen rocked Debbie to and fro. She felt useless with Steven still crying piteously. She endeavoured to divert him.

'Mummy is all right, Steven. She's just fast asleep. Go in the kitchen and get yourself a biscuit and put some milk in your tumbler. When you've had that you can bring some for me.' She was relieved when he did as she'd asked.

Pushing Debbie into a sitting position, she found herself talking non-stop. 'Come on, Debbie. Oh God, please let it only be the drink . . . I know things have been a bit rough, but they can't be that bad. Come on, Debs, it's me, your friend.'

Fay arrived and instantly took charge. 'Doreen, see if there are any lemons in the kitchen, or some Epsom Salts for that matter.' The instructions perplexed Doreen, but she thought it best to do as she was told. After all, she hadn't been able to elicit any response from Debbie herself.

Fay called to her: 'Doreen, come and hold Debbie while I make up a drink for her. Steven, be a good boy and go and sit in your room. Doreen or I will come and see you in a minute. Don't cry now, Mummy will be fine. You go on now so I can help her get better.' As Steven left the room warily, Fay whispered a quick prayer: 'Lord, please help this girl. Make her well and we'll give her the support she needs.'

Together Fay and Doreen moved Debbie into the bathroom. They lifted her on to the cushioned seat of the linen bin and Fay went to the kitchen. Doreen hung on to Debbie as she fell heavily this way and that. Fay returned carrying a tumbler full of a liquid concoction that she began forcing Debbie to swallow. Debbie coughed and choked, then struggled as the liquid reached her throat. At last she opened her eyes weakly and was suddenly retching violently into the sink. Doreen relaxed visibly at this sign of life in her friend, but her own stomach was churning at the acrid smell of the vomit. The retching seemed to go on for ever, but finally Debbie relaxed.

'Take her into the bedroom, Doreen. I'll bring some warm water so you can give her a wash, then I'll tidy up the place. I think she'll be all right now.'

Doreen took the groaning Debbie into the bedroom and deposited her on the bed. She took the flannel and warm water her mother brought and quickly washed her. Then she found a clean nightdress for her friend and covered her with a quilt.

For the first time in a long while, Doreen felt a huge wave of appreciation for her mother. Mum had come to her aid despite the tensions between them. Furthermore, she hadn't even chided her. From the bedroom, she could see her mother restoring the flat to order. Even little Steven was laughing now as her mother teased him and made him feel secure again.

Leaving Debbie to rest, Doreen joined her mother in the kitchen.

'Doreen, do me a favour: ring Sister Taylor and ask her to take my Sunday School class for me, and tell her I'll see her at evening service.' When Doreen returned from making the call, Fay handed her a cup of tea and started to talk.

'You and I need to sit down and talk,' she began. 'Don't look like that!' she added as she saw a dour expression on Doreen's face. 'I know this isn't the time to talk in depth, but I feel that I need to say something *now*. Things haven't been right between us for a while, as you are quite aware. I for one cannot go on living this way without attempting to sort out our differences. You're not comfortable at home with me, I know. So I was thinking you might like to spend some time with your Aunt May. That will give us both some breathing space and time to think.

'Alternatively, I think I'm right in saying that part of Debbie's problem is loneliness. It's no fun bringing a child up alone. Perhaps you could stay with her until she's back on her feet again. It's not that I'm trying to get rid of you: the decision is yours. All I ask is that you let me know what you wish to do. I think it would be in both our interests to be apart for a time. You'll always have a home, whatever

84

happens, with your father and me. We're there if you need us.'

'Oh, Mum. I think I would appreciate that. I've thought about leaving home before, but I didn't know how to raise it,' Doreen responded sheepishly. 'I only wish we could have been this open before.'

'So do I, Doreen . . . So do I,' Fay replied, shaking her head.

Doreen left the kitchen to keep Steven company. But Fay stayed at the kitchen table. A surge of contentment washed over her. She remembered part of a little-known scripture which aptly summed up what she had just been through: ' . . . after that ye have suffered a while, make you perfect, stablish, strengthen, settle you.' Yes, indeed she had suffered and now new strength flowed within her from this step of achievement. God certainly heard and answered prayers!

A Tear and a Sigh
EVADNEY ELLIS

'Mummy, my teacher treats me as if I'm really stupid!'

'What?' said Norma, refusing to accept what she had just heard.

'My teacher treats me as if I'm really stupid!' repeated Kristel-Anne, with a pained look.

With restraint, Norma said, 'What do you mean, darling?'

'If I answer a question in class, she just says, "Hmm", and then asks someone else the same question.'

'But maybe your answer isn't quite right,' replied Norma, 'so your teacher asks another child so that she will be given the complete answer.'

'No, Mummy!' said Kristel-Anne emphatically. 'She does it all the time, and anyway, today my answer was right because Julie gave the same answer as me, and Mrs Dobbs said, "Good girl, that's correct!" and then she gave me a dirty look as if to say, "See Kristel-Anne, you don't count!"'

Norma noted a change in her daughter's expression as her temper fed on the hurt and humiliation she had been forced to suffer. At eight years of age, this child, her baby, was being taught to hate. Kristel's eyes were moist with tears and, as she struggled to control her emotion, the pace of her breathing quickened.

'She's a dragon, and I don't like her!'

Kristel-Anne buried her face in the soft folds of her mother's dress, sucking her thumb for comfort. Battling to maintain control of the storm that was brewing within her own breast, Norma sat down and tenderly lifted her baby onto her lap. Then they held each other, rocking gently.

Eventually she spoke. 'Never mind, darling. Mrs Dobbs is just silly and ignorant. It's people like her who cause a lot of unhappiness in the world, but don't let her get to you: she's not worth it! I know that you are very clever and so does Daddy, so don't bother about her. She's just jealous!'

Norma felt a comforting arm around her shoulder. It was Sonia, her fourteen-year-old daughter. In her preoccupation with Kristel-Anne's problems she had completely forgotten about her other two children. As she looked up, she realized that both Sonia and Daryl were sharing their baby sister's hurt.

As if on cue, both kissed Kristel-Anne, affirming their mother's sentiments about Mrs Dobbs.

That evening, Norma ensured that Kristel-Anne received extra attention from the family. 'We need to show her that we value her,' she had told her other children. To her surprise, Daryl had volunteered to hear Kristel-Anne read, and Sonia had offered to sit with her while she practised her piano pieces. This was a surprise! Normally nothing would have been considered more tedious and unrewarding, as Kristel-Anne was not prone to accept correction or criticism from her twelve-year-old brother or her older sister. In fact, at times, they found her quick repartee quite provocative.

When Earl, her husband, arrived home, Norma related Kristel-Anne's story. Although somewhat upset by the incident, Earl had tried, in his usual way, to play down the issue because he was very wary of 'encouraging a child to harbour negative feelings or thoughts about her teacher', as it could affect their ongoing relationship.

'In the long run,' he said, 'it would be the child who would suffer.' Norma had not chosen to refute this as she knew, from the way she felt, that if she embarked upon any form of argument, she would transfer all the aggression she felt towards Mrs Dobbs on to poor Earl, who really meant well.

During family worship that evening, Norma found herself struggling with her very negative feelings about Mrs Dobbs and her religious conviction that she should pray for her enemies. She winced as she remembered the pained expression on Kristel-Anne's face when she had related her story earlier that afternoon. 'Pray for those who despitefully use you . . .' The words flashed through her mind, leaving a stain of guilt as she tried to focus her mind in prayer. She couldn't remember the last time she had had such difficulty in praying. She had coped with some rather awkward conflicts at work recently; she had coped well with a misunderstanding with her neighbour the previous week.

Reluctantly, she had to admit that she found it easier to cope with offences against herself than with offences against her children. She did not idolize them; in fact, she held firm views about discipline. However, her natural protective instincts were very powerful, and under no circumstances would she allow her children to be made to feel inferior or insecure.

Finally, she forced her lips to utter a simple prayer of submission, saying, 'Lord, I need thee, oh, I need thee, no other help I know. Please touch Mrs Dobbs. Please reveal your love to her, Lord, in the name of Jesus. I ask you to stay close to my children and help them to survive all life's problems. Touch them, Lord Jesus . . . Thank you, Lord, for your help as I submit this problem into your divine hands. Amen! Amen! Amen!'

Yet as she rose from her knees, Norma knew that deep within her heart she had not surrendered the problem fully to the Lord.

The following day she received a telephone call from Rita, her closest friend. They had attended the same schools, worshipped at the same church, and now their children attended the same school. Rita was going to pop in for coffee at 2.30 and then they could walk down to the school together to collect the children. Norma felt grateful for the opportunity to share her thoughts with another mother. They had much in common, and she felt sure that Rita would be able to offer her some sound advice.

Life is so unpredictable, she thought to herself. When they had left school, they had each managed to obtain a place in a highly-recognized university: Rita to read Sociology and Politics at the London School of Economics, and Norma to read English and Philosophy at York. They had both been so excited. They were going to take on the world!

Norma chuckled as she remembered an incident from those days that took place on Clapham Common. Rita had found what appeared to be a sturdy cardboard box and decided to use it as the podium from which she would deliver her maiden speech to Parliament after being elected as the first black prime minister in England. She addressed the trees on the common as the MPs.

'Friends, Romans, Countrymen . . . ' she began in a mocking tone, 'you are highly honoured in having me as your first black prime minister. I promise you wealth, security and stability.' As she said this, the box began to totter. In the next instant the prime minister was flat on her back on the grass, having fallen from her distinguished position without the slightest semblance of grace.

Speaking on behalf of the trees, Norma had said, 'Security and stability. Hear! Hear!' and they had both shrieked with laughter and sheer abandon.

She remembered the time when she and Rita and the other choir members had collapsed with laughter in the vestry after a particularly moving worship service. Rev. Spence had painted a vivid picture of the woman with an issue of blood described in Mark's Gospel, and how she was going to press through despite the crowd and opposition until she touched the hem of Jesus' garment, believing by faith that even one touch would heal her.

Norma began to feel the warmth of the Holy Spirit as she meditated upon this scene now. She remembered how uplifted she had felt as the sermon reached its climax. Suddenly, as a wave of the Holy Spirit seemed to ripple through the church, Norma had felt herself shoot up into the air, shouting. 'Hallelujah! Thank you, Jesus!' she had said as she crash-landed on to her chair.

About a minute later, she realized that she was not sitting comfortably. She elbowed Rita and muttered through clenched teeth, 'Is there a hole in my chair?' Then, easing herself gently to one side, she revealed her chair seat. Rita didn't need to reply. She began to shake with suppressed laughter and had to bow her head in feigned prayer to conceal her face from the choir-master and the congregation. Throughout the remainder of the service, Norma sat bolt upright, expecting at any moment to fall through her chair.

When the service was over, instead of shaking hands with the congregation and greeting them with a holy kiss, Norma propelled herself and the chair into the vestry, hoping to hide it in a corner where it would go unnoticed. Hastily she disrobed. But it was too late. Rita had related the story to the other choir members. Even Norma saw the funny side of it in the end.

Bustling to finish her housework before Rita arrived, Norma noticed that it had stopped raining, and the sudden sunlight seemed to give the room and life a brighter aspect. 'Sleeping on a problem does help,' she thought. 'I don't feel half as bitter towards Mrs Dobbs as I felt last night.'

At 2.15, having filled the kettle and set out two trays, she flopped onto the settee to await Rita. She was listening to her favourite tape of the Florida Mass Choir and sang along with 'I'm so in love with Jesus'. She relished these few minutes of self-indulgence. They were a rare pleasure, for once the children got home she would be into what she called her 'second shift'.

As promised, Rita arrived at exactly 2.30. As a special treat, Norma served rose-hip tea with toasted scones, strawberry jam and fresh cream.

'If Earl could see me now,' she said laughingly. 'He's always complaining about my acquired British taste.'

'Thankfully, I don't have anybody watching my choice of cuisine. We'd probably come to blows,' replied Rita. 'Anyway, mothers should treat themselves once every week in order to relieve the tedium of domestic life. If one week it's ackees and saltfish and the next black forest gâteau, who cares, as long as we're satisfied.'

'My sentiments exactly,' said Norma, as Rita ended her emphatic speech with a flamboyant gesture.

With childish giggles, both women settled comfortably in the lounge to enjoy their hour together.

'So, how's the course coming on?' inquired Norma.

'Girl, it is absolutely up my street,' replied Rita. 'At present we have a visiting black lecturer from the US and we are studying the civil rights movement. Girl, you can imagine how positive it makes all the ethnic students feel, looking at black heroes like Stokely Carmichael, Angela Davis, Marcus Garvey, Malcolm X and Martin Luther King. We really have a heritage to be proud of.'

'It sounds really good,' said Norma, becoming infected by Rita's enthusiasm. 'Do you have a reading list? I wouldn't mind a copy. I'm always thinking that perhaps I should make more effort to keep up my academic interests.'

'That is the understatement of the year!' cried Rita. 'How

many times have I told you to do something for yourself? You can't just live for your husband and children and church. There's more fulfilment to life than that.'

'Yes,' replied Norma good-humouredly, 'but I'm not going to your extremes.'

'Well, maybe not completely, but half way, eh?' chuckled Rita.

Smiling, Norma shook her head and, lifting her hand heavenward, said, 'Touch her, Jesus!'

Then, changing the subject, she enquired, 'How is Rasheed finding life at secondary school? The last time I saw him he couldn't wait to start his second term.'

'Oh, he's loving every bit of it, especially computing and physics. His history teacher has managed to come to terms with his awkward and sometimes embarrassing questions. Last week I took him to see the play *Black Heroes in the Hall of Fame*. It was what you would call an uplifting and positive black experience and it seemed to inspire the entire audience! Well, as soon as we came out of the theatre, Rasheed's questions started. When he went to school the following day, he challenged his teacher by asking why she hadn't told the class when they were doing their projects on the Victorian era that Queen Victoria's great-grandmother was a black woman. About three weeks ago he gave the class a very informative lecture about the black pharaohs of Egypt. They were as black as you and me, Norma!'

'What!' exclaimed Norma. 'I didn't know that!'

'How do you expect to know that when you were taught history within a white racist institution called the British Education system?' Without giving Norma a chance to reply, she continued her tirade.

'Honestly, Rita,' Norma interrupted at last. 'Sometimes you really go over the top. Don't you think I'm aware of racism first-hand? You and your militant friends don't have a monopoly on it, you know. We've all been there. We just deal with it differently. Some of us a little more responsibly than others!'

'Wow!' breathed Rita, somewhat disconcerted by this uncharacteristic outburst. 'What's eating you?'

In the protracted silence that followed, Norma felt a sudden sense of vulnerability as Rita attempted to analyze the harrowed expression on her face. She could feel her heart pounding. She had even begun to perspire. She had surprised herself with the force of her reaction. Obviously, she was more anxious about the relationship between Kristel-Anne and Mrs Dobbs than she cared to admit.

'I'm sorry, Rita,' she said, as her tension eased. 'I've got something on my mind. Please forgive me.'

'Well,' said Rita, 'spit it out. You're always telling me that a problem shared is a problem halved.'

Norma hesitated. She just couldn't cope with another black-activist lecture. She remembered how inspired Rita had been in the early seventies by the Black Power movement. They had heard Angela Davis speak in London and had been captivated by her charisma and the euphoria of the atmosphere in the town hall. Rita had initially subscribed to the views of 'peaceful pro-test' projected by Dr Martin Luther King, but after the burning of the bus in Alabama, she had hardened into a more militant individual.

Unlike Rita, Norma had consciously committed her life to Jesus Christ at the tender age of thirteen. She loved her Lord deeply and had found a totally new perspective on life and relationships. Although she had experienced the oppression of racism, she had not yielded to its cancerous influence.

'Thanks, Rita,' she said, 'but this is one dilemma that I'm going to have to resolve by myself.'

'Well, don't take too long about it,' replied Rita gently. 'It's obviously getting to you.'

The two women spent the rest of the time talking together about less emotive subjects. Norma noticed that Rita's outlook on life had become far more optimistic since she had embarked upon a part-time MA course in multicultural education. She did not seem handicapped by single parenthood; on the con-trary, it appeared to have strengthened her character, enabling her to define carefully-reasoned goals for herself and her chil-dren. She stated quite unequivocally that she had no desire to be 'tied down by any man'. Desmond, the father of her chil-dren, was there to give them a balanced upbringing, not to rob her of her independence. Although she did not agree with her, Norma could understand her reasoning.

The following morning, Norma was awakened early by a violent thunderstorm. Looking at the clock, she realized it was 4 a.m. She snuggled up to Earl, feeling warm and secure. She hated thunderstorms and was grateful to be in bed.

'Mum,' called a feeble voice from the girls' room. 'Mum, I'm scared.' It was Kristel-Anne.

'Earl,' said Norma, 'go and put Kristel-Anne in bed with Sonia.'

'Hmm,' grunted Earl, 'I'm tired, man.'

'It won't take long,' said Norma, giving him an encouraging shove. 'I'll keep your bed warm until you get back.'

Reluctantly, Earl left the comfort of their bed. He knew better than to argue: Norma wouldn't give up, and neither would Kristel-Anne.

Peace restored, Earl stumbled back to bed. As soon as his head touched the pillow, the soft ripples of his gentle snoring wafted around the bedroom.

'Earl,' whispered Norma, trying not to giggle, 'turn onto your side, you're snoring.' He muttered a few incomprehensible sounds and obediently turned over, wrapping his arms around Norma as he did so.

'Perfect!' she thought, as she lay there stroking his hair.

Try as she would, she could not get back to sleep. If it hadn't been for that thunder-clap, she would still be in dream-land. Dozily she lapsed into reminiscence.

Looking at Earl, she reminded herself of how dear he was to her. Yes, it was more than luck: she had actually been blessed with a husband. Earl was the kind of man who was a partner in the true sense of the word. They shared decision-making, domestic chores, financial responsibilities, everything; and they both valued the time they spent together with the children. The fact that they were married didn't deprive either of them of their independence. Their relationship gave each of them the flexibility to develop their individuality.

She remembered a comment made by one of the girls at a

recent youth get-together which they had hosted. Impressed by the natural way in which Earl had helped in the clearing-up operation, the young lady had said, 'Sister Mills, you'd better look after Brother Mills. They don't make men like him any more.' Naturally, all the young men present wanted to shout her down for defaming their characters, but they were outnumbered three-to-one by girls who forced them to do the washing-up. Rita is entitled to her sentiments about marriage, she thought, but I wouldn't have things any other way.

Something that Rita had said did bother her, though. That remark about Norma only living for her husband, children and the church had the alarming ring of truth. Norma felt uneasy. She had always felt sure that her part-time teaching job would keep her mind active and prevent her from vegetating, but sadly she had found that it offered very little stimulus. She didn't really want to take on a serious course of study until the children were a little older. After all, she had chosen to have them and she had a responsibility to do her best by them. However, there in the deepest recesses of her mind existed a haunting shadow called 'secret aspiration', which was waiting to surface. The temptation to resign from teaching had appealed to her for some time now, but the convenience of being able to have holidays at the same time as the children had outweighed other considerations.

Allowing her mind to wander, Norma had visions of herself as a successful working mother at the helm of her own business. She would sport the professional 'Harrods' look, with its tailored suits, and flaunt the ostentatious cut of the hair that said very loudly, 'I am the business woman in control!' She would change her spectacles for a pair that added an air of distinction, and the final touch would be the soft leather accessories that would indicate a woman of taste, class and means!

As she mulled over these secret ambitions, her pleasure was tinged with guilt for craving such material, temporal fulfilment as opposed to the delicate, eternal, pious virtue of cultivating the inner self and those spiritual attributes she so admired.

She ought to want only the virtues that would bud and flower into the satisfaction of knowing that she was a devoted mother to her children, a loving wife to her husband and a bastion of the church community who would provide divinely-inspired counselling to the other brethren. What is it to be, Lord? she thought.

Another thunder-clap jarred her back to reality. The rain was falling even more heavily now. Without disturbing Earl, she crept over to the window and peered surreptitiously behind the curtain. Her childhood fear of being struck by lightning surfaced momentarily, but maturity prevailed. As she stood in the dim dawn watching the angry raindrops falling like bullets on the fresh young leaves of the lime tree at the front of the house, she drifted again into deep thought. It was as if her inner dilemma was being staged before her eyes. The pummelling raindrops symbolized the raging conflict in her mind. Different inclinations were being shot down the moment they emerged. What was she to do with her life?

What was she to do about Kristel-Anne's problem?

Suddenly, there were several powerful gusts of wind. She watched the large frame of the tree resist their compelling force. After each gust the branches seemed to reassert themselves, as if resolved not to be moved.

Suddenly, all was calm.

Gradually, sunlight peered over the horizon. The branches of the tree oscillated gently in the light, refreshing breeze, and all of nature seemed relaxed as Norma's thoughts transcended its tranquillity. Had her thoughts, needs and present emotions been embodied in that tree? Was it showing her how to weather situations of conflict and confusion?

'Lord,' she smiled, 'you do speak in mysterious ways.'

The peace and quietness of spirit that she had derived from this early-morning meditation lasted for several weeks. In fact, life appeared so problem-free that Norma suspected it was the calm before a storm in her own life. She remembered the words of dear Mother Franklyn, 'Brethren, Satan give me a break last week, but this week him try to bounce me down. I called to

Jesus and the Holy Spirit catapult him and him drop like a dead fowl, and now I am standing on victory ground!' Had Satan taken a break merely to round up his forces for a concerted attack? Shrugging off these thoughts, she decided to luxuriate in the serenity while it lasted. Relishing her secret desires had boosted her self-esteem. She paid extra attention to her appearance, styling her hair more frequently. She applied herself more enthusiastically to her teaching, and the pupils responded by doing excellent work. She felt wonderful. Positive thoughts were producing positive results.

About four weeks after this, Norma noticed one evening that Kristel-Anne was particularly quiet and thoughtful. This sudden change in demeanour was so pronounced that even Earl noticed and made considerable effort to coax her into conversation. He was unsuccessful. Most of her responses were monosyllabic. During dinner, Kristel-Anne kept eyeing Daryl furtively, and whenever their eyes met she would quickly avert her head. Daryl found this quite amusing and shared the joke in a whisper to Sonia. As they both sat there giggling, the furrows in Kristel-Anne's forehead deepened until eventually, with a cool, long stare, she said, 'Daryl, have any of your friends ever been in trouble with the police?'

'Who wants to know?' responded Daryl, teasing.

'I'm not joking!' retorted Kristel-Anne crossly. 'Just answer my question, please.'

Responding to a threatening look from his parents, Daryl said, 'No, why do you ask?'

'I just wondered,' came the curt reply.

After what appeared to be a lengthy silence, Kristel-Anne turned solemnly to her parents.

'Most black men don't grow up to be muggers and thieves, do they?' she asked. She was so intense that it seemed she was willing them to say no.

'Of course not, darling,' said Earl. 'Where did you get such a silly idea?'

'Jamie said it in class today.'

'He must have been joking or just trying to tease,' responded

99

Earl, in an attempt to defuse the growing intensity of the conversation.

'No, Daddy,' retorted Kristel-Anne. 'He was perfectly serious, and I didn't like it!'

She blinked hard as she fought back the tears. Her whole body seemed charged with emotion. To Norma it seemed as if, for Kristel-Anne, her entire race and identity were being questioned in one destructive statement.

Very gently, Earl said, 'OK, darling, take your time and tell us what happened today. Start from the beginning.'

'This afternoon, Mrs Dobbs showed us a film about young people getting into trouble. It was about a black man who was brought before a judge for mugging an old lady. Then there was another story about a white man who had committed frauge . . . '

'Fraud,' corrected Daryl.

'Fraud, then,' repeated Kristel-Anne grudgingly. 'Then we saw another black man who was a thief. The judge had to listen to all their stories and then decide what punishment he would give them. While we were watching the film, Jamie kept looking at me and Sherell, who's the only other black person in the class, and kept giggling. Afterwards, when the class was discussing the film, he kept trying to make the class laugh by saying nasty things about blacks that his parents have told him.'

'OK, darling,' interjected Earl, 'we get the picture. Now, what did Mrs Dobbs say when he said those things?'

'She tried to hide her smile by trying to look cross. Then, in a deep voice, she said, "James!" But he just ignored her, and she didn't do anything.'

'I see,' said Earl.

'Yes, and that's not all,' ranted Kristel-Anne. 'Just before home-time, he kicked me as he walked past my chair, and when I told Mrs Dobbs, she just said, "And what were you doing, just sitting there like a silly wally, or were you trying to trip him up?" But, Daddy, I wasn't doing anything!'

'I know,' responded Earl, visibly moved by his daughter's anguish. 'Come here, baby.'

Lifting her onto his lap, he held her close and patted

her gently. He understood her pain, her confusion and her resentment of blatant injustice. His mind produced a sudden flashback of his own early experiences.

There he was, running home from school, half-blinded by tears. At the age of ten he had just had his first encounter with overt racism. He had only been in England for about four weeks and was enjoying the novelty of his new environment and the strange culture where they ate 'Irish potatoes' in so many different forms. On his third day at school, he had felt the tingle of achievement when he had been able to give the correct answer to a question in class. He had been vaguely aware of the startled look on the teacher's face and the bewildered look on the faces of some of the English children who had answered the same question incorrectly; however, he had not allowed that to cloud his triumph.

Travelling home that evening, he had decided to celebrate by spending his threepence pocket money in the posh-looking sweet shop on Newington Green Road. On entering the shop he had been so absorbed in his private thoughts that he did not notice the hostile look directed at him by the shopkeeper. He walked over to the counter and selected his favourite sweet. Just as he was about to pick it up, a harsh voice boomed, 'Get your black hands off my sweets!'

He remembered the sudden numbness he had felt as his hand hovered above the chocolate bar, suspended by those words. Looking up, he saw the small, cold blue eyes set in an otherwise pleasant face staring down at him.

'We don't want no blacks in 'ere,' continued the voice.

He had left the shop in a daze. The tingle of earlier success was replaced by the hammer of rejection. He had not been prepared to deal with this kind of experience and had walked, stumbled, then run semi-blindly the rest of the way home. When his parents had arrived home from work, they had found him in a fretful sleep on their bed, the pillow drenched with tears.

Wiping away Kristel-Anne's warm tears, Earl assured her that, between them, he and Norma would do something to resolve her problem.

101

It was the first time Norma had stood aside in any situation regarding her children and allowed Earl to deal with it without her involvement. It had been a very difficult thing for her to do. Whenever there was a crisis, the children would usually turn to her. Gradually it had become her automatic responsibility to resolve problems, simply reporting the result to Earl. This time she was attempting to apply a different strategy. Earl can deal with this, she thought to herself. I don't think I can trust myself with Mrs Dobbs this time.

As they discussed the matter in bed that night, Norma vented her anger on Earl, accusing him of passivity. So he suggested sending a letter to Mrs Dobbs outlining their concern about the incidents that had occurred. This way, he felt, they would not jeopardize Kristel's future relationships with staff within the school.

'You of all people should know,' she stated, 'that professionals close ranks whenever there is any sort of threat to a colleague. A letter can be misconstrued, and we could end up being labelled as the offenders, without having our case vindicated.'

After much discussion, Norma resentfully accepted the fact that they both employed different tactics in solving problems of this nature. She concluded that, on this occasion, Earl's assistance could turn out to be a handicap. She was more aggressive and more assertive, and she was convinced that Mrs Dobbs would respond better to her approach. Finally, she concluded that this situation had to be resolved by her.

The following morning, Norma telephoned the school to make an appointment to see the headmaster. She discovered that he was away on a two-week course and would not be available in school. Sensing the disappointment in Norma's voice, the secretary said, 'You can see Mrs Holman, the first deputy, this afternoon.'

'No thank you,' replied Norma. 'I'll wait until Mr Daniels returns.'

Replacing the receiver, Norma reflected on the excessive politeness the school secretary always showed towards her. She had suspected that she was not in the habit of meeting black

102

middle-class parents. In fact, on her initial visit to the school, Norma had recognized a distinct note of surprise in the secretary's reaction when she introduced herself as Mrs Mills.

'Oh yes,' the secretary had mumbled, as she fumbled through the pages of the school diary.

'I did make an appointment to see the headmaster,' Norma had said. 'I'm surprised that you weren't expecting me.'

'Oh, but we were,' had been the nervous reply. 'Ah, here you are, Mrs Mills: 2.30 p.m. with Mr Daniels.'

'Yes,' Norma had responded with a penetrating stare.

She had watched the colour in the woman's neck change from cream to vermilion as the wave of embarrassment had swept over her. It reminded Norma of the chameleon she had once goaded when she was a child in Jamaica. It also had changed colour as a result of a direct confrontation with her.

'Do take a seat, Mrs Mills. I will let the headmaster know that you have arrived.'

As she had taken the seat proffered, she had watched the chameleon scuttle off into the headmaster's office, changing colour yet again as it went.

On Wednesday evening, Norma surprised the family with an announcement: 'I'm going to the prayer meeting tonight.' She had anticipated Kristel-Anne's response exactly.

'Oh, Mum, do you have to go? I haven't had you all day, and you need to hear me read.'

'Dad can hear you read tonight,' replied Norma. 'I need some food for my soul, so you will all just have to do without me.'

'But we need you,' Kristel-Anne persisted.

'Leave Mummy alone, Kristel-Anne. Don't be so selfish. I don't want Mummy to go either, but she needs some time to herself,' interrupted Sonia with an air of maturity. 'Mummy hardly ever goes anywhere.'

'That's right,' said Norma playfully. 'What do you want to do to me, Kristel? Make me your prisoner?'

Directing her reply to Sonia, Kristel-Anne skilfully avoided Norma's question. 'I wasn't speaking to you, big mouth. I was talking to Mummy. You don't like me butting into your conversation, so please don't butt into mine. I just love Mummy.'

Unable to contain himself any longer, Daryl giggled with amusement as Sonia groaned her response. Even Norma wanted to laugh, but she knew that Kristel-Anne would be mortally wounded by such indifference.

As she switched off the ignition, Norma heard the chimes for seven o'clock on the radio. 'Perfect timing,' she thought. Whenever there was a house prayer meeting, the ladies would arrive early to enjoy fellowship and to help prepare the refreshments for afterwards. Tonight was no exception. As she rang the bell on Sis Hetta's front door, the inviting smell of baking and the cheering sound of women's laughter reached her. Verna, Sis Hetta's teenage daughter, ushered Norma straight into the kitchen, which was alive with activity.

As Norma entered she was greeted with warm, affectionate smiles and some friendly surprise. Unable to conceal her pleasure at Norma's arrival, Mother Franklyn, who though frail in body had a sprightly sense of humour, embraced her with a big hug and kiss and then proceeded to dance on the spot, singing, 'Sis Norma come to prayer meeting, what a blessing tonight, my Lord!'

After recovering from her amusement, Norma said, 'If this the type of welcome I get for coming to a prayer meeting, I think I'll come more often.'

'Sis Norma, come and butter some hard-dough bread for me. I have to work you now that you're here.'

'My pleasure,' said Norma, downing her bag and washing her hands. As she joined the other ladies preparing the food, Norma exclaimed in surprise, 'Mercy! Look at food! Sis Hetta, what are you planning to do to my waistline tonight?'

'Waistline!' laughed Sis Hetta, holding her corpulent hips. 'I've been looking for mine for the past ten years and I haven't found it yet!'

Sis Hetta was noted for her cooking and tonight she had prepared a variety of delectable West Indian fare. There was fried fish to go with the hard-dough bread, stuffed roast beef, jerked pork, fried dumplings, ackee and salt-fish, roti, patties, several varieties of salads, sweet-potato pudding, cornmeal pudding plus several other cakes and an enormous bowl of tropical fruit punch.

'Surely all this food isn't just because of the prayer meeting, Sis Hetta. Is there something you're not telling us?' asked Norma, eyeing her suspiciously.

'Lawks, Sis Norma,' exclaimed Sis Hetta, pinching Norma playfully. 'Your lickle mind is too quick.'

'But stop,' said Mother Franklyn thoughtfully. 'You are quite right you know, Sis Norma. Now that you mention it, she really has gone to town tonight. I am not folding any more serviettes till she tells me the secret!'

With that, Mother Franklyn placed herself in a chair in front of Sis Hetta and sat there staring into her face expectantly.

Poor Sis Hetta, cornered as she was, started to giggle with embarrassment. Five pairs of eyes waited expectantly for her reply. Suddenly, in the suspense of the moment, Sis Tiny remarked, 'Eh, eh, Hetta blushing!'

That did it. Everybody simply convulsed with laughter as poor Sis Hetta fanned herself in an attempt to cool her now musk-pink cheeks. Indeed, a deep blush suffused her sandy neck, and she was powerless to conceal it.

'OK!' she said, when the laughter subsided. 'I didn't want to tell you until the prayer meeting had started, but as I have no choice,' and here she stared hard at Mother Franklyn, who was still chuckling, 'I'll tell you now. Today is my forty-sixth birthday, so this prayer meeting is really a thanksgiving to God for keeping me all these years.'

'I knew something was up,' said Norma, as everyone started hugging and kissing Sis Hetta. 'You should have told us so we could buy you a present.'

'No, man,' replied Sis Hetta. 'It is enough just to share this special evening with my family and the family of God.'

Having finished setting out the food, they joined the other guests, who were seated in Sis Hetta's homely lounge. As she sat there, Norma observed that the décor and soft furnishings were what she would describe as typically West Indian. The walls were hung with burgundy flock wallpaper, which matched the deep-pile patterned burgundy carpet. Family photographs were affectionately displayed in large frames hung on the wall, and the former, slimmer Sis Hetta smiled serenely down on the occupants of the room.

The suite was covered in cream leatherette and consisted of a large five-seater settee, a three-seater settee and two inviting recliners. Against the back of each seat rested a circular red velvet cushion, carefully arranged to give additional comfort, and behind these hung crocheted chair-backs, which had been so popular with Norma's mother's generation.

The centre-piece of the room was the large onyx coffee table decked with a skilfully-crocheted white swan stiffened with starch, around which was arranged a flock of cygnets with little red bills. The neck of the swan served as a holder for a large vase, which contained an artistic arrangement of flowers. In the alcoves stood two ornate glass cabinets, the one on the left displaying Hetta's best china, and that on the right, her best crystal.

I wonder if she has ever used them? thought Norma, as she remembered her own mother's insistence on displaying the 'best' wares in the cabinet in their lounge.

The homeliness of the environment helped to generate a feeling of warmth and unity. When they prayed, Mother Franklyn's rich and vibrant voice could be heard above the others as their potent faith propelled them closer to God in thanksgiving and worship. Norma felt an increasing lightness of spirit as she harnessed the joy and exuberance that pervaded the atmosphere. The climax of the meeting came when Sis Hetta stood to give a vote of thanks to everyone for sharing in the meeting.

"'The Lord is my rock, my fortress, and my deliverer: my God my strength, in whom I will trust; my buckler, the horn of my salvation, and my high tower, I will call upon the Lord, who is worthy to be praised: so shall I be saved from my enemies." Like David, I can say these words with conviction, because for forty-six years I have proved God. There have been times when I have felt as if I couldn't make it. The pressures and cares of this life seemed set to press me down, but in his divine mercy

Jesus reached out his hand and rescued me.' She paused as her voice quivered with emotion, and supportive 'Amens' echoed around the room.

'I remember the time when, after innumerable tests, my doctor advised me to give up hope of ever bearing children because of the risk of their being born with sickle-cell anaemia. I fasted and prayed for seven days and then God told me to wait. Brethren, I waited!' Reaching over to grip her husband's hand she continued, 'We waited and trusted and tonight we give special thanks for our two children whom God miraculously blessed us with. Neither of them has inherited the illness.'

For a moment all eyes focused on Verna and her ten-year-old brother, Keith. Their normal reaction would have been to cringe with embarrassment when identified publicly, but tonight they lovingly shared their parents' emotion. Trembling, Sis Hetta concluded, 'I have so much to give thanks for that it would take me all night to tell you, but I will agree again with David who in commitment to God said, "Thou shalt guide me with thy counsel, and afterward receive me to glory." Continue to pray for me, brethren, for I mean to go to heaven.'

Before Sis Hetta could regain her seat, Verna and Keith stepped forward with a bouquet of deep red and white roses. 'Mum, this is to say we love you,' whispered Keith, as their father joined in, embracing Sis Hetta affectionately.

'What a wonderful evening!' said Mauva, as she entered Norma's car. 'Sis Hetta's family generate such genuine affection towards each other that one just can't help loving them.'

'Hm!' agreed Norma dreamily. 'I know that prayer meetings are uplifting, but tonight's meeting was something special!'

'Yes, I'm glad I came. Normally there are only about fifteen of us, but tonight was a really full house. By the way, what prompted you to attend tonight, Norma? You're not one of the midweek regulars, are you?'

'You're right,' replied Norma, smiling thoughtfully, 'I'm not. I just felt in need of this kind of fellowship tonight, plus the fact that I'm praying about a particular matter — know what I mean?'

'Well, I understand the need,' responded Mauva sympathetically. In the brief pause that ensued, Norma wondered how Mauva found the time to attend so many midweek meetings when of her four children the eldest was only eight.

'Anyway, how's the family?' she enquired.

'Exhausting!' groaned Mauva.

'The baby must be a big man by now. What's he doing for himself?'

'Too much,' chuckled Mauva. 'He's able to take six steps before toppling over now, and has discovered that talcum powder looks good on the carpet and in his hair!'

'Goodness!' squealed Norma in amusement. 'Wait till he discovers what he can do with Vaseline. That's when he'll have a field day. When Daryl was a baby he gave me such a fright. One morning I left him alone in my bedroom for about five minutes and returned to find his head and face absolutely covered in a combination of Vaseline and powder. To crown it all, as I entered the room the little urchin gave me the broadest grin and scampered away from me as fast as his hands and knees would carry him. It took me ages to clean him up.'

'Thanks for the warning,' Mauva laughed gratefully. 'I must make sure that everything's kept well out of reach!'

'Anyway, how is Madame Kristel-Anne? She must be ruling the roost now that she's all of eight years.'

'You are definitely a discerner of spirits, Mauva,' Norma exclaimed. 'You should see her in action. Sometimes I literally have to leave the room. Just last Tuesday, Daryl asked her to return a book that she had borrowed from him, but he omitted to say "please". "Ask me properly," came Madame's gruff retort. "OK. Please can I have my book, Kristel-Anne," he repeated humbly. "Don't whine!" was the curt reply, and she strutted off, leaving him standing there. Poor Daryl. Naturally, we insisted on an apology, but in private Earl and I simply collapsed in hysterics.

'Seriously though,' continued Norma, as she decelerated to make the journey last longer, 'we've had to give her a lot of extra emotional support since she entered Mrs Dobbs' class.

That woman's racist innuendos are sapping the poor child's confidence, and there's no telling what long-term damage it's doing to her. I don't see why, when black people are contributing so much to the nation's economy, our children should be forced to experience the same bigotry that we endured.' As she spoke, Norma fancied that she sounded like an echo of Rita's militancy.

She recounted the recent events involving Mrs Dobbs and waited expectantly for Mauva's reaction, hoping for some positive suggestions about how to deal with her quandary.

'Poor child!' breathed Mauva. 'I suffered a very painful experience at the hands of a teacher that I shall never forget. It was soon after I started attending primary school in this country. In Guyana I had been considered of average ability, but my forte was reading and spelling. When I started school in England, they treated me as if I was retarded. One day I was presented with the ideal opportunity to prove my ability to the class. With this, I thought, they would surely be forced to accept me as one of them. But it wasn't to be — the teacher saw to that.

'He asked if anyone knew how to spell the word "Mississippi". With great enthusiasm I shot my hand into the air, but the teacher just ignored me and kept asking other children to try. I held my hand up for such a long time that eventually it began to feel tired and heavy. Gradually his blatant rejection forced it down. I remember biting my lips to hold back the tears. Suddenly he turned to me and said with disdain, "Yes, Mauva?" Despite my shock, I spelt out the word confidently and correctly. "Not quite!" he announced. "She's nearly there, but not quite."

'To my disgust, a boy put his hand up. "Yes, James?" said the teacher. In his clear English tongue, James proceeded to say, "M i double s i double s i double p i." The teacher said "Excellent!" as James sat down with a look of triumph.'

Norma could feel a lump developing in her throat as she listened to Mauva's moving account of this traumatic experience.

'From that day onwards, I never ever attempted to answer

109

any of the questions that that particular teacher put to the class,' concluded Mauva.

'Dear God,' sighed Norma. 'Why do black people suffer so?'

As she pulled the car up outside Mauva's house, Norma said despondently, 'I don't know what I'm going to do about Mrs Dobbs, but one thing is sure: she is going to have to change.'

Resting her hand on Norma's arm, Mauva tried to reassure her. 'It is the plan of the enemy,' she uttered. 'Satan is trying to discourage you, but prayer is the key. I'm glad you came to the meeting tonight because I'm sure that God is working on this problem already.'

'Well, when I get up to that school I'll be working on it too,' came Norma's firm reply.

'No!' objected Mauva. 'God doesn't need your help. Leave him to deal with it in his own way.'

'I don't believe I'm hearing you right, Mauva. This isn't some problem that we can spiritualize and ignore until it goes away. It's a human problem that God has given us wisdom and logic to resolve in human terms. God helps those who help themselves.'

'Well, I always take all my problems to God in prayer, and he always solves them for me,' insisted Mauva. 'That way you avoid battling with other people. I know how hard things sometimes seem for us. After all, if you compare the price of yam to the price of potatoes you have to admit that it's even more costly to be black.' Norma was amazed at this flicker of perceptiveness in Mauva, but it had been only momentary.

'But these things will only endure for a season on this earth, Norma,' continued Mauva as she stepped out of the car. 'Remember that our eternal home is over yonder.'

'Oh yes,' replied Norma softly. 'Give my love to the family. 'Bye.'

As she drove off towards her own home, Norma felt numbed. Despite the fact that she and Mauva were peers, their outlook on life was completely different. Whereas Norma knew herself to be a realist, Mauva's sensibilities were shrouded in the shadowy vale of escapism. She was incapable of dealing with difficult or unfavourable issues with their real-life context. After all, it's so much easier to blame Satan for our failures than to admit to our own shortcomings, thought Norma.

'Earl!' called Norma, bolting the front door. 'Do you want some supper. Sis Hetta sent you a piece of fried fish, hard-dough and cake.'

'Yes, please!' replied Earl. 'I'll have the lot plus some hot chocolate.'

'You would!' laughed Norma. She went into the kitchen, emerging a few minutes later with a well-laden supper tray.

'How was the meeting?' enquired Earl.

'Oh, it was wonderful!' came Norma's enthusiastic response. 'That Sis Hetta is really cunning. She wasn't just having a prayer meeting; it was also a thanksgiving for her forty-sixth birthday.'

'So she took you all by surprise, did she?' laughed Earl.

'Not quite. We gave her as good as she gave us,' giggled Norma, as she proceeded to relate how they prised the truth out of Sis Hetta while causing her maximum embarrassment. Earl found this highly amusing.

'Who else attended the meeting?' Earl enquired.

'Everyone!' exclaimed Norma. 'The Jordans, Bakers, Grants, Walters, St Claires, Jones, Sis Hill: I can't list them all, but I would say there were about thirty to forty people altogether.'

'Anywhere there is food the vultures gather,' said Earl mischievously.

'Really!' responded Norma, slapping him playfully. 'Oh, guess who else was there? Bro and Sis Engles,' said Norma, lapsing into another fit of giggles. 'That poor man looks so hen-pecked it's unbelievable. Poor man, I do feel sorry for him. Mind you, he shouldn't allow his wife to be so domineering.'

'But surely she's just a typical Church of God wife,' said Earl provocatively.

'I'll thump you,' Norma replied, attacking him. 'Some church women may be like that, but I'm not.'

'No, you're not,' cried Earl, attempting to shield himself from Norma's tickles. 'You're gentle, kind and loving.'

'That's right,' said Norma, smiling menacingly as she withdrew somewhat breathlessly. She knew how ticklish Earl was and she was prepared to exploit the weakness, even if it did exhaust her.

'I gave Mauva a lift home,' began Norma after she had recovered her breath.

'How is she? I haven't seen her for some time.'

'Quiescent and boring!' sighed Norma. 'In fact, mentally she is becoming a replica of Sis Ella.'

'What do you mean?'

'I mean she is mentally stagnant, immobile! She doesn't seem to think for herself any more. She just seems to sit there accepting dogma, conforming to tradition and generally doing what people expect of her.'

'Perhaps she is happy as she is. Surely that's what counts.'

'But Earl, what about her poor children? Firstly, she is obviously not teaching them about the Christian faith in an objective way, and secondly she spends most evenings attending every meeting that is being held at church, so she is not even fulfilling her maternal role adequately.'

'Hmm!' agreed Earl. 'It's an easy mistake to make — some people go out to meetings all the time and then they wonder why they can't communicate with their children when they become teenagers.'

'Well, that's what I mean,' came Norma's intense reply. 'How many young people have we counselled who have admitted to us that they can't communicate with their parents, and when you examine the matter more carefully you find that the parents are so busy attending church meetings that they have simply forgotten to bring up their children "in the fear and admonition of the Lord" as they promised so sincerely at the christenings.'

In the ensuing pause, Norma made a mental analysis of the community in which they lived. She burned up inside as she stumbled upon the realization that some Christian parents did not have the positive relationship with their children that some parents who didn't conform to a particular religion had achieved.

'What really peeves me,' concluded Norma, 'is the fact that Mauva and I are peers. We grew up together, yet her outlook is a complete antithesis to that of the modern woman. I see now why Rita described her recently as the "personification of the social and economic repression of the status of women."'

'Don't be too hard on her,' said Earl, switching on the news in the hope of diverting Norma's attention.

'Well, she is,' insisted Norma, suddenly aware of her own ranting. 'OK, I'll stop talking now, but just let me say this: if Mauva cannot connect praying to doing then she has missed out on one of the main themes of the Christian message — faith with works!'

'Amen!' muttered Earl as he settled back into the comfort of the cushions to watch the news.

At work the following day, Norma received a note from the headteacher saying that she was expecting a visit from Tracey Gore's parents and that they had requested that Norma be present at the meeting. Norma was somewhat bemused at their request, but as the head was arranging for a cover-teacher to relieve her of the lesson with the notorious 3C, she had no objection whatsoever.

At 2 p.m. precisely, Norma knocked at Miss McBride's door. The green light above the door flashed, signalling for her to enter.

'Ah! This is Mrs Mills,' said Miss McBride, introducing her to Mr and Mrs Gore.

'How d'you do, Mrs Mills,' said Mr Gore, shaking her hand. Mrs Gore just smiled shyly at Norma. They were both older than she had expected, and it was obvious that Tracey, their only child, had been born in the autumn of their marriage. Mrs Gore looked timid and lacking in confidence, and Norma wondered how she coped with a recalcitrant child like Tracey. Mr Gore was of medium build, with a distinctive red beard. Something about him said quite clearly that he was the ruler in his house.

113

Miss McBride explained that Tracey had again been playing truant from school and that her parents had also discovered that she was involved in solvent abuse. Although they had tried to persuade her to get proper medical help, she had repeatedly refused, saying that they didn't really care about her and that using solvents was her only way of relieving the monotony of her life.

As Miss McBride spoke, the couple sat as still as statues. Mr Gore was staring hard at the floor, while Mrs Gore was crying silently into her handkerchief.

Norma listened, trying to work out why she was being told all of this. After all, she thought, I'm not Tracey's form tutor. I only teach her twice a week, when she decides to turn up.

'Tracey has told her parents that you are the only person whom she trusts, because you are the only person who tries to understand her,' announced Miss McBride.

'Me?' said Norma, almost pinching herself to see if she was dreaming. 'I don't understand.'

'Yes, Mrs Mills,' said Mrs Gore softly. 'Yours is the only homework she ever does, she really likes you.'

'Well,' replied Norma thoughtfully, 'I suppose I have spent a considerable amount of time talking to Tracey about her work and about herself, but I had no idea that it meant so much to her.'

'I have noticed,' Miss McBride said, 'that whenever Tracey gets into trouble in school, she generally heads either in your direction — or out of the school gate.'

'I suppose she does,' conceded Norma. 'But where is all this leading?'

'We, that is, my wife and I, are wondering if you'll come round and 'ave a word with her, miss. She just won't listen to anyone else,' pleaded Mr Gore.

'If you think it would help, I'd be only too happy to,' replied Norma sympathetically.

'I feel obliged to point out that Mrs Mills is under no professional obligation to do this,' said Miss McBride, looking pointedly at Norma. 'I don't want her to feel that she has to go.'

'Thank you, Miss McBride, but I wouldn't be happy to live

with myself if I didn't at least try to talk to Tracey,' responded Norma.

'Good!' she replied smiling. 'I'm glad you feel that way.'

They arranged for Norma to make an informal visit the following Monday at seven o'clock.

I'll buy Tracey a little gift, she thought, as she drove out of school later that afternoon. How ironic life is! Here I am, a black teacher, battling with a white racist teacher who is trying to damage my own daughter's prospects by eroding her self-esteem; yet I'm giving up my own time to help a white child. Why should I care? It's just that I do.

As she drove over the heath to Kristel-Anne's school, Norma remembered the last conversation she had had with Tracey. She remembered the expression of loneliness and confusion on the child's face and her own struggle to find the right words to say to her. Recently she had begun to suspect that Tracey had suffered some emotional problems and she had wondered whether or not the girl's parents were aware of this. Tracey had also exhibited extreme insecurity with male teachers and had started to play truant from their lessons. Who'd be a teacher? Norma asked herself, shaking her head.

The first thing Norma did each Monday morning was to check her appointments diary for the entire week. This Monday was no exception.

'Earl, remember that I'm going to visit a pupil tonight, so do hurry home, darling.'

'OK, love,' he replied, kissing Norma goodbye.

The day went well for Norma. All her classes brought in their homework, and some of the pieces seemed very promising. As she would be free during the last lesson, she planned to mark as many books as possible in school, in order to minimize the number of books she would need to take home with her.

As she was dismissing her last class, she noticed the headmistress hovering outside her classroom. Norma observed, with some amusement, the unusually quiet and orderly way in which the pupils walked in single file down the corridor. It was obvious that the name 'McBride' had been whispered in warning, especially to the infamous 3C who were going into the library across the corridor.

'Can I see you in my office in about five minutes, Mrs Mills?' asked Miss McBride, putting her head round the door.

'Certainly!' replied Norma, with affected willingness.

'Bang goes my marking!' she muttered to herself, as Miss McBride closed the door.

As Norma settled herself into the large, comfortable armchair in Miss McBride's room, she wondered why she had been summoned yet again.

'I received a very distressing call from Mr Gore about half an hour ago,' began Miss McBride. 'Apparently Tracey has been glue-sniffing again, only this time the consequences have proved to be rather grave.'

'What's happened? Is Tracey all right?'

'Not quite,' replied Miss McBride, obviously trying to deliver the news as sympathetically as possible. 'I know this will come as a great shock to you, but I have to tell you now. Tracey attempted to commit suicide today by throwing herself into the path of a double-decker bus.'

'Oh God!' breathed Norma, as a deathly chill crept over her body. A frostlike fear suddenly gripped her heart as she asked, 'She will survive, won't she?'

'The doctors aren't sure,' came the reply. Norma involuntarily locked herself in the world of her own sombre, private thoughts. What can have happened to push poor Tracey down this slippery slope? Why has she done this? Why didn't she come to see me? Oh God, what can I do now? Is it already too late? The questions came fast and furious.

'Are you all right, Mrs Mills? Mrs Mills, are you all right?'

Norma was only vaguely conscious of the headteacher's presence and was too shocked to respond. Mechanically she accepted the cup of sweet, black coffee that Miss McBride placed carefully in her hand. The warmth of the coffee helped Norma to regain some of her lost composure. As she returned the empty cup, Miss McBride said, 'Tracey has been placed on a life support machine at St Leonard's Hospital. Her parents have said that you are welcome to visit should you wish to do so.' Realizing how much the news had affected her, she placed her hand sympathetically on Norma's shoulder.

'Thanks for telling me,' replied Norma as she returned to reality. 'I would very much like to see her.'

'I think perhaps it would be a good idea if you went home a little early today. Do you think you'll be able to drive, or shall I ask someone to run you home?'

'Oh no!' said Norma softly, 'I'll be fine, thank you very much.'

Leaving the head's office in a stupor, Norma walked straight to the car park. She just couldn't face anyone right now. Tears of regret flowed inwardly as she walked down the corridor. In her mind she was screaming, *No, God, no! You can't let her die!*

'Miss, are you all right?' came a blurred enquiry from a pupil.

Norma hurried by silently, unable to muster the inclination or the composure to reply.

She reached the car. Like an automaton, she pushed the key into the lock, turned it, opened the door, sat behind the steering wheel and then slammed the car door shut: she was shutting out the world.

At last she was alone with her grief. The force of the emotion within her breast propelled her body forward until she was slumped over the steering wheel. Gradually the painful tension that had built up inside her began to release. It was like the thaw after a long, hard winter. Her muscles relaxed and her body began once again to feel. First came the tingling sensation like that of an anaesthetic wearing off, then came the torrent of unrestrained tears: tears of deep sorrow for Tracey.

When she eventually managed to regain some composure, Norma found herself mulling over the many unresolved questions and inner conflicts that Tracey had ventured to share with her over the last year in which she had been her confidante. Suddenly these questions assumed a new significance. Their expression had not been a part of her catharsis. They were not the catalyst that led to a reformed character. They had simply preceded the violent upheaval in her life. Now all at

117

once, they seemed to hang silently in the air, tinged with crimson and pulsating with grief, still unanswered.

The alarm on her watch trilled, reminding her that it was the end of a school day. The sound brought her abruptly back to reality. As she started the engine, Norma realized that she had no recollection of how she had got from Miss McBride's office to her car. Her actions had been quite mechanical. Her mind had been totally obsessed with thought about the devastating impact of some enigma that now had Tracey straddling the canyon between life and death.

As she rounded the corner to Kristel-Anne's school, Norma noticed that two children from her daughter's class had already reached the main road. She was late. As she parked near the school gates, she saw Kristel-Anne leaping down two steps at a time in order to get to her.

'Hello, darling!' she said as Kristel greeted her with her usual kiss.

'Hello, Mummy,' replied Kristel-Anne. 'Why are you so late today?'

'I'm not that late,' retorted Norma playfully. 'Anyway, something came up at school.'

'Oh,' said Kristel-Anne understandingly, before launching into a detailed account of the day's events while Norma chauffeured her home.

Later that evening, as the family chatted together at the dinner table, Norma felt a heightened sense of appreciation for her family and for life. As she watched each of her children, she felt a sense of pleasure in their individuality and youth. Her opportunity to help Tracey might have gone, but she still had the chance to help her own children. Inwardly she felt a renewal of her zeal to fight to give them the best opportunity to succeed in life, despite the Dobbses of this world.

'Mummy, it's Wednesday today. Don't forget to come to our open afternoon; and, Daddy, don't forget to leave work early to get there on time,' said Kristel-Anne excitedly. 'I've made you both a "welcome" card and I'm sure you'll like it. I wrote a little poem inside it.'

'I can't wait to see it,' said Norma smiling. 'Now hurry and finish your breakfast or you'll be late for school — and so will I.'

As promised, Norma met Earl outside the school gates at exactly 3.30. On the way to Kristel-Anne's classroom they stopped to look at the display work in the corridors and were highly impressed by the quality of the children's work. Passing by a group of paintings about weddings, they noticed that there was only one of a black couple. On looking more closely they read the name 'Kristel-Anne Mills' underneath the picture. Norma smiled with satisfaction. Despite the constant flow of negative messages that Kristel's teacher conveyed about race and culture, Kristel had developed a strong self-concept that enabled her to project her social and cultural identity in her art. Mrs Dobbs had not succeeded in destroying that!

When they entered the classroom, Kristel-Anne's face lit up. Bursting with pride, she carefully guided them around the room, giving a running commentary on all the work displayed on the walls and the clay models made during their weekly activity sessions. Whenever she came to a piece of her own work, she would take some time to explain the thought behind its creation.

As they looked through her classwork books, Kristel exhibited profound interest in her work, surprising her parents with the depth of understanding she had developed. Norma and Earl smiled as they came to a book entitled *About Me*. In it she had written about herself from before birth to the present day. They noticed with considerable amusement that Kristel-Anne had substituted intimate family details with some rather plausible fancies. Their lifestyle, as projected in her book, was much more lavish than in reality but, as Kristel-Anne explained to her parents, 'I didn't want *her* to know too much of our business!'

During the hour they had spent in the school, they noticed Mrs Dobbs circulating among the parents. She appeared quite friendly and charming in this setting, despite her reputation among the children as 'the teacher who shouts the most'.

'Odd, isn't it?' muttered Norma as they left. 'She only managed to say "hello" and "goodbye" to us.'

119

'Never mind,' responded Earl, placing a comforting hand on her shoulder.

'Daddy, did you like my work?' came an anxious question.

'Like it!' exclaimed Earl. 'I loved it! My daughter is the cleverest girl in the world. In fact, I think she is almost as clever as me!'

'Oh, Daddy!' replied Kristel-Anne, striking him playfully as she buried her blush in the folds of his jacket. 'Be serious!'

'All right, I'm serious,' said Earl, standing to attention as he passed his hand over his face in an attempt to wipe the smile away. 'My name is General Serious. Attention! Well, I'm generally serious anyway.'

'Ugh!' shuddered Norma laughing as Kristel-Anne chased her father to the car. 'How corny.'

Throughout dinner that evening, they talked only of the open afternoon. Both Norma and Earl expressed praise and encouraged their daughter to work hard because what they had seen of her work was positive proof that she was endowed with a high level of intelligence.

'All you need to do is to work hard at your spelling,' counselled Earl. 'That seems to be the only area in which you need help.'

'And in mathematics,' added Kristel. 'I don't know my nine-times table yet.'

'OK,' said Norma decisively. 'I intend to give you a lesson every evening during which we'll concentrate on spelling and number-work. But you must promise to work hard. Should I have to go out at any time, Daddy, Daryl or Sonia will help you. Agreed?'

'Agreed,' responded Kristel-Anne contentedly, failing to notice the grimace on Daryl and Sonia's faces.

Norma had made an appointment to see Kristel-Anne's headmaster, Mr Daniels, on the following Monday afternoon. Norma hoped that he would have been exposed to some multicultural input at least once during the two-week course from which he was returning. She was convinced that

120

he would benefit from it. Whether he had or not, she had come to the conclusion that he would sooner or later have to face up to the problems being experienced by black children in his school. He can't bury his head in the sand for ever, she thought.

Since the day of Tracey's suicide attempt, Norma had made up her mind that, regardless of the consequences, she would no longer allow Kristel-Anne to suffer at the hands of Mrs Dobbs. She had concluded that children had only their parents to defend them and if the parents failed to do so the children would be at the mercy of the worst human instincts. Tracey, only gradually recovering, was a tragic reminder of this.

Greeting Mr Daniels with a confident handshake, Norma decided to be the dominant personality in this meeting. She chose to sit on an upright chair that placed her on equal eye-level to Mr Daniels and she proceeded to make small talk.

'Did you enjoy your course?' she enquired.

'Oh yes,' Mr Daniels replied in his distinctive Scottish accent. 'It was very pleasant indeed. The conference centre was in North Wales. The air was clean and the scenery breath-taking. However, like all good things it had to end.'

Norma smiled. 'I understand that the title of the course was "Changing Thought in Primary Education". How drastic are the changes as perceived by headteachers?' she enquired casually.

'Too drastic, if you ask me,' he began. 'Why should we make all these changes to the structure of our curriculum when it has worked so well in the past? And now they are introducing some fancy new job descriptions to bring advisers into schools to update staff on the new concepts of a "balanced curriculum".'

'But isn't that a good thing from the schools' point of view?' questioned Norma. 'Surely it can only benefit staff? If they have access to resources that will broaden and bring more relevance to the curriculum, won't the pupils in turn benefit?'

'I don't know about that,' countered Mr Daniels, 'but what I do know is that money that should be channelled into education for all pupils will be spent providing resources for a small group, and I don't see how that can be justified. I've been teaching for thirty-five years now, and regretfully I shall have to work for another three years before I become eligible for early retirement. I think it is an affront that people like myself should be expected to change our methodology after all these years in the service. Anyway, I'll get down off my soap-box now, Mrs Mills. I'm certain you didn't come to see me simply to discuss my course.' He smiled. 'What can I do for you?'

Having probed his mind, Norma knew the type of strategy she would need to employ. Judging by the views he had just expressed, he had a tendency to bigotry.

'Well, Mr Daniels,' Norma began, 'I have come to see you about a long-standing problem. My husband and I have tried to avoid making an issue of it, but we now feel that the cost of continued silence is too great. We feel that it could have a devastating effect on our daughter's confidence. It appears that Mrs Dobbs' treatment of black children and race issues is not in keeping with your stated anti-racist policies.'

'That is a very serious allegation, Mrs Mills,' interjected Mr Daniels uncomfortably. 'I've known Mrs Dobbs for a number of years, and she has never indicated any strong feelings about race or colour. Perhaps there is some misunderstanding.'

Norma felt her temper rise, but she breathed deeply, held it at bay, and continued.

'How can you attempt to absolve her when you have not heard details of the complaint?' she questioned calmly. 'I would not waste my time coming here if I didn't have grave cause for concern.'

'Do continue,' he acquiesced.

Beginning with the most recent incidents, Norma proceeded to describe the numerous occasions on which Kristel-Anne had complained about the way her teacher treated her. She vividly depicted the times when Kristel had tearfully reported scenes of rejection and isolation, concluding with the statement 'Mummy, I don't want to go back to school'.

As she spoke she could see that her words moved Mr Daniels, but that he didn't know how to manage the situation. Again, he reacted defensively and attempted to play down the implications of what Norma had related.

'Mrs Mills,' he began assertively, 'I have been headmaster at this school for the past fifteen years. Mrs Dobbs has been here for the last five years. She has taught white, coloured and Asian children, and I have never had any complaints from any of their parents about the way she treated them. In fact, it was only last month that a very troublesome ex-pupil called Desmond Jackson visited the school. He's coloured and he exhibited no hostility whatsoever towards Mrs Dobbs, who had been his teacher during his last year here.'

'That is not the issue,' objected Norma firmly. 'I'm not interested in her track record. I *am* concerned about what she is doing to my daughter *now*. Anyway, in the past black parents have been extremely reluctant to come into what is to them the alien environment of British schools in order to complain.'

Mr Daniels looked fearful, as if there was a sudden danger of all his years of service being analyzed and rejected.

'I have always worked hard to cultivate an ethos within this school in which children and parents of all nationalities would feel welcome,' he retorted. 'In fact, it was that same ethos that appealed to you when you first brought your children here, Mrs Mills, so how can you expect me to countenance such an allegation against a member of my staff?'

Norma felt as if rocket boosters had colluded to fire her temper. It wasn't just Mrs Dobbs who had a problem: Mr Daniels also had one — a blind spot! Sitting squarely on her chair and discarding the strategy of caution, she embarked upon a speech that would prove to be her emotional catharsis.

'Mr Daniels, I can see that you are simply not aware of the needs of black children, so I will forgive your apparent ignorance. My three children have attended your school, and in the ten years that I have been in contact with this institution, you have not seen the need to recommend to the governors the appointment of even one teacher from any ethnic minority. This is despite the fact that twelve per cent of your annual intake of pupils is Afro-Caribbean or Asian. I know of several suitably-qualified applicants who were rejected at interview. You pride yourself on the ethos that you have cultivated within the school. It is indeed praiseworthy, but where are the positive role-models for children from ethnic minorities? The only one I've seen is the cleaner who had to be employed under section eleven in order to justify the receipt of the Home Office grant.

'You have just spent two weeks discussing changing thought in primary education. Hasn't it made you stop and think about the absence of multiculturalism from your school curriculum? When you do topic work on things like tolerance, worship and sharing, you could easily introduce multicultural resources. But no: it would mean, to quote your own words, "spending money which should be channelled into education for all pupils on resources for a few". Yes, a few blacks.'

'Well, really, Mrs Mills. This outburst is quite intolerable. I appreciate that you are upset about Kristel-Anne's situation, but it does not provide grounds on which you can simply walk in here and make unsubstantiated allegations. Only last month we had input from a group of African dancers at a talent evening. You witnessed that yourself. Even you will have to admit that I am beginning to introduce community groups into the school.'

'Yes,' replied Norma, 'and what an anachronism! At a time when we should be bonding the community by helping our children to perceive the equality of all people, you bring in one African dance group which by itself only serves to reinforce the negative stereotype of blacks being primitive and only capable of performing ritual dances.

'How many of the audience appreciated it as a developed art form? I sat very close to Brigadier and Mrs Houghton-Hall and observed their response with interest. The brigadier applauded patronizingly at the end of the act while his wife sat stiff and upright, peering down her nose with disdain. Why didn't you invite a black classical musician, or poet or artist?

'With all the good intention in the world, you in your white skin, Mr Daniels, cannot appreciate what it really feels like to be black. You need to talk to black people and try to see life through their brown eyes. Then, and only then, can you begin to think about meeting true multicultural needs.

'I have sat through several assemblies in this school and not once have I heard you refer to black or Asian people to illustrate your talks. The only exceptions have been when you have made appeals on behalf of a charity, and even then the images

124

projected are of millions of poor starving blacks in squalid conditions. I don't deny that these scenes are realistic, but where is the balance? Not all black people live like that!'

'I'm quite certain we are all aware of that fact, Mrs Mills,' Mr Daniels prevaricated. 'I don't think that is a fair comment.'

'It may not be fair, but it's true,' Norma replied, still trying to repress her soaring anger. 'I remember how inadequate my own education was in preparing me to face the truth about Jamaica. You see, I went through the first half of my life identifying Jamaica and Jamaicans with the huts and shanty towns that I had seen in the films at school in England. I had grown up thinking that was the norm. When I was in my late teens I returned to Jamaica for the first time since the age of five. Can you imagine my amazement when I discovered that most Jamaicans live in spacious bungalows with colourful, well-kept gardens? And they aspire to do better for themselves! The curriculum being offered to my daughter almost twenty years later is still reflecting the same negative values and low standards. Introduce balance, Mr Daniels!'

Norma could see that at last she had managed to make some impact. He sat like one gradually emerging from hypnosis. Norma could tell from his eyes that he was re-evaluating his long experience as a teacher in the light of what she had said.

Norma continued in a more subdued tone: 'If you were talking about football hooliganism, you might well balance your presentation by showing that the majority of spectators in the stands are far more controlled. In the same way, when talking about crime in the community, you should take care to ensure that delinquent blacks are portrayed as a small minority and provide illustrations of the positive role of the majority of blacks. We don't want to take over; we just want to be accepted for what we truly are.'

As the conversation developed, Norma felt her soul begin to breathe and her passion to subside. Mr Daniels had begun to listen and to hear more of what she was saying and he gradually withdrew his defensive blockade.

Closing the door on Norma shortly afterwards, Mr Daniels walked slowly over to his large armchair and gently draped himself over it. He felt benumbed. Never in his life had he envisaged having to live through the scene that he had just experienced. In his state of shock, he needed a pause in which to reflect.

He had never felt any great compulsion to consider these issues in depth, and now they had been thrust upon him without any warning, propelled from the perspective of an individual inside black skin. The experience had touched the exposed nerve of his Christian conscience. Somehow he felt that his future appeals during Christian Aid Week for the starving in Africa would have an empty ring to them unless he made a mammoth attempt to address the needs of the black children in his own school. No longer could he feel that his appeals discharged his obligation to God.

What has Eleanor Dobbs started? he thought to himself. He couldn't deny the feeling of rancour that accompanied his thoughts about her. Her xenophobia had now placed him and all his staff in an invidious position.

Arriving home with Kristel-Anne, Norma felt intoxicated with success! She had surprised herself with her forthrightness during the meeting with Mr Daniels. But she had to admit to herself that, when roused, she could command the devastating force of Hurricane Gilbert. As she watched Kristel-Anne doing her homework, she cherished a sanguine hope for her future in the school. She had now issued a challenge to the sinister purveyor of racism and she felt sure that, when informed of the fact, Mrs Dobbs would suddenly become very vulnerable and very human.

Two days before the interview evening, Kristel-Anne stunned the family when she announced, 'Mrs Dobbs said my work was very good today, and she actually smiled at me!'

Daryl and Sonia couldn't believe their ears.

'Are you sure she didn't mistake you for someone else?' asked Daryl jauntily.

126

'Oh no, I made quite sure that she was speaking to me,' rejoined Kristel-Anne.

'She's running scared,' thought Norma menacingly. 'She ain't seen nothing yet.'

'Don't raid the larder,' called Norma to her children as she left with Earl for their interview with Mrs Dobbs. 'Daryl, please remember that Sonia is in charge while we're out, so no arguing.'

'Yes, Mum,' replied Daryl reluctantly.

When they arrived at the school, they found that a considerable number of other parents had arrived early.

'The black parents are conspicuous by their absence,' whispered Norma to Earl.

'I thought you knew better than to expect them to turn out in force,' replied Earl sceptically.

'Yes, but one does live in hope,' concluded Norma, and she smiled across the hall to Dr and Mrs Jacobs.

As they waited, Norma occupied her mind by trying to analyze the facial expressions of people emerging from the interview rooms. It was not difficult to distinguish the faces of parents who had received unfavourable reports about their children's progress and behaviour during the past year.

Norma felt a sudden palpitation as Mr Daniels approached them. She hadn't expected to see him tonight. He shook hands firmly, inviting them into his office for 'a brief word'.

'Mrs Mills, our recent conversation forced me to do a great deal of thinking and painful heart-searching,' he began cautiously. 'Following this, I made certain proposals to staff, as a result of which I have now instituted a new policy for dealing with future racist or sexist incidents. Each parent will receive a letter informing them of this, but I wanted to present yours personally. After you have had a chance to read it, I'd welcome your comments.'

As they resumed their seats outside the interview room, Norma read the letter. 'Listen, Earl!' she said excitedly. Quoting from the letter, Norma continued: '"All racist or sexist incidents are to be reported to me and must be recorded

127

in the large yellow book housed in the General Office. Entries will be dealt with immediately and all reports will be carefully monitored. Appropriate action will be taken in all cases. Signed, A.G. Daniels, Headmaster".'

Norma was stunned! She hadn't anticipated this! Mr Daniels had risked losing popularity with some of his staff and parents in order to respond to the needs of a minority. How wrong she had been about him. She had been too quick to stereotype him as a racist. He had merely been a victim of his own ignorance.

Leaning back on her chair, Norma closed her eyes and exhaled long and steadily. Her bitterness evaporated, dissipated of energy. Her feeling of triumph was clouded with guilt. She reproached herself for being so fired by fury that she had failed to think in a Christian way. Her original motive of simply wanting to make Mrs Dobbs more aware of Kristel-Anne's needs and the plight of other black children had been obscured by a desire for revenge. She hadn't allowed for divine intervention. Yet now she realized that she had benefitted from it.

'Forgive me, Lord,' she breathed.

'Mr and Mrs Mills, Mrs Dobbs will see you now.'

The secretary's voice jolted Norma into the present. She felt like one who had been snatched from the edge of a precipice. She had thrown down the gauntlet, and Mr Daniels had responded positively to the challenge. The battle was now over, and it was time for constructive dialogue.

As she approached the interview room, Norma lifted her thoughts in prayer: 'Lord, please give me the words that I should speak.'